Wild about Weston

THE ENGLISH BROTHERS, BOOK #5
THE BLUEBERRY LANE SERIES

KATY REGNERY

Happy Reading to Judy! ♡ Katy, Wes & Molly xo

SPENCER HILL PRESS

Please visit www.katyregnery.com

First Edition: December 2014
Katy Regnery

Wild about Weston: a novel / by Katy Regnery—1st ed.
ISBN: 978-1-63392-076-7
Library of Congress Cataloging-in-Publication Data available upon request

Published in the United States by Spencer Hill Press
This is a Spencer Hill Contemporary Romance, Spencer Hill
Contemporary is an imprint of Spencer Hill Press.
For more information on our titles visit www.spencerhillpress.com

Distributed by Midpoint Trade Books
www.midpointtrade.com

Cover design by: Marianne Nowicki
Interior layout by: Scribe, Inc.
The World of Blueberry Lane Map designed by: Paul Siegel

Printed in the United States of America

The Blueberry Lane Series

THE ENGLISH BROTHERS

Breaking Up with Barrett
Falling for Fitz
Anyone but Alex
Seduced by Stratton
Wild about Weston
Kiss Me Kate
Marrying Mr. English

THE WINSLOW BROTHERS

Bidding on Brooks
Proposing to Preston
Crazy about Cameron
Campaigning for Christopher

THE ROUSSEAUS

Jonquils for Jax
Coming August 2016

Marry Me Mad
Coming September 2016

J.C. and the Bijoux Jolis
Coming October 2016

THE STORY SISTERS

Four novels
Coming 2017

THE AMBLERS

Three novels
Coming 2018

Based on the best-selling series by Katy Regnery,

The World of...

The Rousseaus of Chateau Nouvelle
Jax, Mad, J.C.
Jonquils for Jax • Marry Me Mad
J.C and the Bijoux Jolis

The Story Sisters of Forrester
Priscilla, Alice, Elizabeth, Jane
Coming Summer 2017

The Winslow Brothers of Westerly
Brooks, Preston, Cameron, Christopher
Bidding on Brooks • Proposing to Preston
Crazy About Cameron • Campaigning for Christopher

The Amblers of Greens Farms
Bree, Dash, Sloane
Coming Summer 2018

The English Brothers of Haverford Park
Barrett, Fitz, Alex, Stratton, Weston, Kate
Breaking up with Barrett • Falling for Fitz
Anyone but Alex • Seduced by Stratton
Wild about Weston • Kiss Me Kate
Marrying Mr. English

For anyone who's ever met "the one" at a wedding
With thanks to Melinda and Mandy for
naming Molly McKenna and to
Rachelle, who handed
me "Dusty" on a
silver platter

TABLE OF CONTENTS

Chapter 1

Molly McKenna loved her family, friends, and her parent's beagle, Lady. Asked to name three more things she loved, on any random day, she might answer:

1. Watching her students get excited about reading.
2. The smell of fresh-cut wheat straw.
3. Weddings.

When Molly left her home in Ohio and took a job as an English teacher at a middle school in downtown Philadelphia, she knew it was going to be an uphill battle to get her students interested in literature. And yet, after six months of teaching, she had learned that while the rewards were intermittent, they were also more satisfying than she could have imagined. The first time her class got into an organic debate—arguing whether or not the characters in *Ninth Ward* should have stayed put or evacuated during Hurricane Katrina—the rush was more powerful than anything Molly could have imagined.

The smell of fresh-cut wheat straw, which she—regrettably—hadn't had the opportunity to whiff in almost eight months, reminded Molly of her family's farm in Hopeview, Ohio. Hay baling, which typically took place in June, reminded her of the warm sun, longer days, the end of the school year, fresh squeezed lemonade, and her mother's famous blueberry pie, which won the blue ribbon at the county fair almost every year. It reminded her of innocence and laughter, high hopes and sweet dreams. Yes, indeed. Better than Christmas trees or pumpkin bread or burning leaves in the fall, fresh cut hay was Molly's favorite smell on earth.

And because Molly was a die-hard romantic, devouring romance novels like popcorn, and a veritable expert on every rom-com movie released from 1986 to the present, she loved weddings. She loved being in weddings, she loved attending weddings, she loved the parties, showers, and teas that led up to the big day. She loved thoughtfully choosing the perfect gift for the bride and groom. She loved the way the church smelled of fresh flowers, and she was an unapologetic and unabashed wedding-crier.

When "Here Comes the Bride" swelled on the church organ, her eyes glistened as the groom's face invariably softened with awe and devotion at the first glimpse of his bride. Molly's tears fell when the father-of-the-bride's voice broke while giving his baby girl away. If the minister used Corinthians I in his sermon, Molly was a total goner, softly saying the verses right along with him. She sniffled and wiped her eyes again as the vows were exchanged and rings blessed . . . and like any other true-blooded romantic, she wept like a spring rainfall when they kissed, then beamed like summer sunshine when they were pronounced man and wife.

Yes. On any random day, Molly would include weddings on her list of three things she loved.

Just not today.

Definitely *not* today.

Molly rolled over, batting at her blaring alarm clock until she haphazardly managed to hit the snooze button. Desperately trying to hold onto sleep, she clenched her eyes shut tightly. It didn't help. The warm numbness of slumber slipped away too quickly and a terrible heaviness descended, squeezing her heart and compressing her lungs as more tears—impossibly—filled her still-burning eyes.

"Still-burning" because she'd flown over Ugly Cry Land sometime last night around nine o'clock, and she was fairly certain that if she looked in the mirror, her bloodshot eyes and pale skin would be well into Walking Dead territory by now.

"That's what you get for six straight hours of crying, dummy," she sniffed, blinking her eyes furiously as if it would help. It didn't.

Her cat, Charming, jumped on her bed and meowed softly before mercifully lying down and purring loudly beside her ear in a passive demand for breakfast. She flipped onto her back and glanced at him before staring at the ceiling.

"I shouldn't have picked up the damned phone, Charming," she said, pressing the heels of her hands against her eyes. She tried to take a breath through her nose, but between last night's cry-fest and waking up to more tears this morning, she was good and clogged up.

"Maybe I'll e-mail Daisy and tell her I've come down with something awful. Or, no. I'll call her and leave a message. She'll hear it in my voice."

Charming opened his eyes and stared at her accusingly, his expression neatly conveying the thought *Liar, liar, pants on fire*.

Using her very worst swearword, she exclaimed, "Christ on a cracker, I don't want to go to a wedding today! Is that so hard to understand?"

The big, old, melon-colored tomcat stared at her for an extra beat and then yawned, never taking his eyes off hers. His ennui was unmistakable—he couldn't care less that her woman's heart was in turmoil; she'd already RSVP'd yes.

"Oh, fine, I'll go. Darn it, but you're mean," she said, whipping off the covers and swinging her legs over the side of the bed. "But I'm not going to act happy. No, sir."

Taking a ragged breath, she sternly admonished herself to ignore whatever tears still felt like falling, and resolved to move through her day as though her heart hadn't been broken in half at approximately seven-o-six last night.

Looking straight ahead, Molly's eyes scanned the framed photos on her dresser: her parents on their wedding day, Molly with her sister and two brothers on the tractor, Molly wearing her graduation cap and gown, Molly standing with a class of minority students against a brick wall covered in heavy graffiti, then a big empty space where two additional photos had resided until last night. She bit her bottom lip, jumped up, and rearranged the remaining four photos to take up the space now vacated, glancing into the trash bin where the other two had met their untimely end.

It didn't make her feel better.

She hoped a long, hot shower would.

Molly did her best thinking in the shower, and right now she needed to think of a way to get through the day: to show up at Daisy Edwards's four o'clock wedding—*stag*—and make it through the ceremony and reception in one piece. Outwardly only, of course. Inside, the million shattered pieces of her mangled heart would still be jagged, still be aching, still need time to heal from the hurt and embarrassment and shock of last night's phone call.

She padded into the kitchen with Charming trailing behind and poured him a bowl of cat food, then lifted his water dish and refreshed it. There was comfort in the mundane—feeding her cat, watering the little herb garden on her windowsill, turning on her coffee maker. It all made her feel more normal, less like her world had been punched in the throat last night.

Stripping out of her pajamas, she turned the shower hotter than usual and stepped inside the stall, letting the water beat down on her aching body.

When Dusty's number had popped up on her phone last night, she assumed he was calling to give her his estimated time of arrival. He was driving from Hopeview to Philly so that they could spend Valentine's Day together and attend Daisy's wedding.

Though Molly and her fiancé had drifted apart a bit over the past six weeks since they'd last seen one another over Christmas break, it was only because they were both so busy. Dusty was working hard on setting up a new PE program at the Hopeview Junior High School, and Molly was almost halfway through her first year of teaching at-risk kids in a low-income neighborhood of Philadelphia.

When Molly had decided to take the two-year teaching job with Teach for America, they'd both known it would test their relationship, but she'd convinced herself there was nothing to worry about. Whenever they saw one another, they jumped right back into their relationship and everything went back to normal.

Back to normal because it hadn't escaped her notice that their weekly phone conversations had become much shorter, stilted, and mechanical lately—more an information swap than the communion of two people deeply in love. And sure, for the past few weeks, Dusty had sort of glided over the "I love you" at the end of the call, answering "Yup, you too" and hanging up quickly instead of returning the actual words. But heck, all couples had ups and downs, didn't they? Dusty was still her fiancé, and this weekend would've been their much-needed chance to reconnect.

Yeah, right.

"What a fool you are, Molly McKenna," she whispered to herself as she squirted bath gel into her hand. A sharp pang of grief and panic suddenly overwhelmed her. She let the gel drip forgotten through her fingers and took a gasping breath of steam as she recalled their conversation.

"Hey, Valentine!" she'd answered cheerfully. "You pass Harrisburg yet?"

"Uh, no Mol. We need—"

"Pedal to the metal, baby," she said. "I'm waiting for you! Got a big box of candy with your favorite centers and—"

"Molly! Stop for a minute. We need to talk."

"Is everything okay?" Her heart had kicked into a gallop, suddenly on high alert from the dark tone of his voice.

"No. Everything's not okay."

"Dusty, you're scaring me. Are you sick? Hurt?"

She reached for the TV remote and turned off the program she was watching so she could give him her undivided attention.

"Jesus, Molly, I don't know how to say this, so I'm just gonna rip away the Band-Aid real quick, okay? I've been seeing Shana Evans since Thanksgiving and she's, uh, she's having a baby."

The first thing Molly realized was that she wasn't breathing. It was like someone had thrown a rubber ball down her throat and closed up her windpipe.

The second? Her hands were trembling so hard, her phone shook against her ear.

The third? The entire contents of her stomach were about to dislodge that little rubber ball.

She barely made it to the nearby kitchen sink in time, dropping her phone to the counter with a clatter and retching into the basin. Gagging over the smell and the sour taste in her mouth, she threw up again before reaching for the faucet. Dispensing with a glass, she stuck her mouth under the tap to suck up some water and rinse out the sink.

It was several minutes before she picked up her phone again.

"Dusty?"

"Molly? You there?"

"Dusty," she said quietly, looking at the oven clock. Seven-o-six. Her eyes flooded with tears and the numbers blurred into distorted, white zigzags as she walked slowly from the kitchen and fell heavily onto her couch. "What did you do?"

"Christ, Mol, are you okay?"

"No. No, Dusty," she sobbed. "I'm a long, long way from okay. What . . . what are you t-talking about? How did Shana—"

"Listen, baby—"

"No!" she exclaimed, her nostrils flaring in defiance as hot tears trickled down her cheeks. "I'm not your 'baby' anymore."

"*Molly*," he said, and her free hand fisted as she heard the hint of indignance in his voice, as though perhaps Molly was partially to blame for what had happened. "You've been gone for eight months. *Eight months*."

"*So what*?" she exploded. "So that means you can *bake cookies* with the art teacher? That means you can cheat on the woman you're marrying?"

Molly pictured Shana Evans—her trying-too-hard, bleached-blonde hair and beady, calculating eyes. Growing up in the same small town, Molly had known the Evanses all her life. In fact, Joel Evans had asked Molly to the eighth grade formal once upon a time and she'd said no because he gave her the willies. Forcing her thoughts back to the present, she gasped as the truth hit her square between the eyes and she had a brief, but revolting, mental image of Dusty and Shana in bed together. "Oh, my God, she's pregnant? She's *pregnant*, Dusty!"

Molly couldn't say why it had taken this long for her to absorb the fact that Dusty was having a baby with Shana Evans, but fresh tears deluged her eyes and she took the phone away from her ear for a second, trying to catch her breath.

When she held the phone back up to her ear, Dusty was mid-sentence. ". . . growing apart for a long time now. I missed you something awful at first Molly, but hell, we only slept together but once over Christmas, and you—"

"Wait," she gasped. "W-Wait," she said again, her brain trying hard to piece together two parts of the conversation. "*When* did you get together with Shana?"

"Wh-what?"

"*WHEN DID YOU START SLEEPING WITH HER?*"

"Aw, Molly."

"Oh, my God! You said it before . . . Thanksgiving. Thanksgiving, Dusty. You started getting *with her* around Thanksgiving and you were *with me* at Christmastime."

"N-Now, Molly. That's an ugly accusation—"

"Accusation? It's a fact, Dusty! From your own mouth!"

For the first time since they'd started talking, she looked down at the simple engagement ring on her finger. When Dusty had proposed after their graduation from teaching school in June, the little diamond glistening in the sunshine had easily been the most beautiful thing she'd ever seen. Now it seemed like a symbol of cheating, pain, and stupidity. She wrestled it off her finger and flung it across the room, watching as Charming jumped off the couch in pursuit.

"Well, Mol, I don't know what else to say. You took that job in Philadelphia, even though there was a perfectly good position open at Hopeview High, and—"

"You knew how important Teach for America was to me, Dusty! You knew it was my dream!" she sobbed.

"Well, it wasn't *my* dream! *You* were my dream. *You*, Molly. You and me staying here, raising a family near where we grew up, Sunday dinners with the folks, going to the same church where we—"

"You go near that church and lightning will split your head open before you can step through the door!"

Dusty was silent for a long time. "We're not getting anywhere, Mol, just throwing around nasty words we'll regret. Let's talk another time when you're not so upset—"

"*Words we'll regret*? Dusty, I couldn't give a . . . a . . ." She tried to think of the most vulgar curse words she overheard every day in the hallways at school. ". . . flying f-fucking cock's *shit* if you don't like the words I'm using. I hope you are monumentally unhappy with Shana Evans. I hope she cheats on *you*. I hope *you* get to learn how it feels. I hope . . . I hope—"

She stopped abruptly. The line was suspiciously silent.

"Dusty? *Dusty*?"

The line was dead. Somewhere during her foul-mouthed tirade, he'd hung up on her. *He'd* . . . hung up . . . on *her*. Molly had thrown the phone across the room, but this time Charming ran for cover as she let out a long, keening sob, and fell to the floor on her knees.

Happy *fucking* Valentine's Day.

Molly rested her forehead against the mustard-yellow tiles in the shower as the hot water continued to scorch her back. She reached for the cold water tap, twisting it just a touch. The water mellowed a little, and she reached for the gel again.

He'd cheated on her. Her boyfriend of ten years—a wasted *decade* of her life—had cheated on her. And how. Aside from the pain of his betrayal and rejection, her embarrassment was epic. Everyone in Hopeview would know Dusty had dumped Molly for Shana, and they'd quickly learn the sordid reason why.

"Oh, God," she moaned, rubbing the gel over her body distractedly.

What would her parents say? What about her older sister and two older brothers who still lived in or around Hopeview and still attended the same Methodist church as Dusty every week? Had Dusty even had the decency to tell Molly first? She mulled over this question and decided that yes, he had. She'd checked her phone this morning after finally charging it, and there were no calls or texts, so it was safe to assume Dusty told her first. Her phone would be ringing off the hook once her friends and family found out. And sure, they'd all feel bad for poor Molly, but good Lord, she'd look like a fool who couldn't hold her man. Not to mention, there would be some who'd say she had it coming, up and leaving a handsome young buck like Dusty Hicks behind.

She shampooed her ginger-colored hair and thought back to Christmas break. When she'd first gotten home, he'd come to see her, but every time Molly had tried to talk about her life in Philly or his in Hopeview, he'd silence her by kissing her, which had finally led to them having sex in the back of his car. As she thought back on it, yes, Dusty had been distant with her, canceling two dates and rushing through gifts with her family on Christmas Eve. When she asked where he needed to be, he said he needed to help set up the church for the nine o'clock service, though it was strange to Molly at the time, because although she'd looked for him, she didn't recall seeing him at the actual service.

Now it occurred to her . . . he was probably leaving her to go see Shana, which begged the question: Who was this man who used church as an excuse to get it on with his piece-on-the-side? She thought she knew Dusty Hicks as well as one human being could know another, but she was wrong. She didn't know this cheating, lying piece of scum at all. And more hurt, angry tears ran down her cheeks to mix with the hot water still pouring from the shower head.

"You'll need to get tested," she whispered miserably, wringing out her hair and watching the water run clear. Because Dusty was her fiancé and Molly was on the pill, they'd never used any protection. And if Shana was pregnant, he certainly hadn't been using condoms with her. She shook her head in disgust and fury.

Good Lord, what a disgusting excuse for a man.

Thankfully, the realization of Dusty's epic selfishness had the counter-effect of staunching her tears for the first time since waking up, and her jaw was set in an angry line when she turned off the water and stepped from the shower.

Wrapping a towel around her small frame, she rubbed a circle in the steam on the mirror and finally looked at herself. Her cheeks were bright red due to the hot water, but so were her eyes. After whipping the medicine cabinet open, she took out a small plastic bottle of Visine and tilted her head back, letting three or four drops fall into each eye. Screwing the top back on, she opened her eyes wide and watched as they cleared a little, one stray tear making its way down her nose to rest on her top lip. She snaked out her tongue and licked it.

"That's the last tear I cry for you, Dusty Hicks. That's a promise."

Then, still heavy-hearted despite her bravado, Molly marched into her bedroom to throw on some clean underwear, grateful she still had several hours to psych herself up for the very last place on earth she wanted to be: Daisy Edwards and Fitz English's Valentine's Day—ugh—wedding.

Chapter 2

Weston English took one last look around his apartment, feeling like he was forgetting something. Tuxedo? *Check*. Gift? *Check*. Keys? *Check*. Toast? He patted his breast pocket, but it was bare. He ran back to the desk in his bedroom and rifled through legal documents and various law books until he found the piece of paper he'd printed out late last night: his wedding toast to his brother, Fitz, and his fiancée, Daisy, who were getting married today. Weston and his three other unmarried brothers were all planning to say a few words.

More than a little bleary-eyed from studying until three o'clock in the morning, he shook his head and grabbed his half-finished coffee cup off the dining room table as he passed. He downed the remaining dregs in a gulp and placed the cup back on the table, reminding himself that after he passed the bar in two weeks he wouldn't need to keep burning the midnight oil studying. Checking his watch, he realized he still had forty-five minutes before he had to pick up Constance Atwell, his on-again, off-again girlfriend and date for Fitz's wedding.

He grabbed the dozen long-stemmed red Valentine's roses from his refrigerator and ran through the checklist in his mind again, satisfied he wasn't forgetting anything.

Pulling his black overcoat out of the small front closet, he pictured Connie naked as he closed and locked the door behind him, making the decision to pick her up early. Maybe he'd catch her coming out of the shower, and she'd be up for a quickie before driving out to Haverford. Weston grinned at his reflection in the brass wall of the elevator, his body tightening a little in anticipation. Connie was always horniest right before social events, a fact Weston knew because he'd often been the beneficiary of her favors at such times.

Heading out the front door of his modest apartment building located near the University of Pennsylvania, Weston hailed a cab and gave the driver Connie's address.

With his four brothers in serious relationships and Weston's second-oldest brother, Fitz, getting married today, Weston turned his thoughts to his relationship with Connie.

Weston had known Constance Atwell for most of his life. The Atwell sisters had grown up in the same area of Haverford as the English brothers, and they'd attended the same country club, hunt club, dance school, and Catholic Church. While Weston's mother, Eleanora English, and Charity Atwell weren't the best of friends, the Atwells had certainly been invited to the annual English summer party every year.

The crossover hadn't ended there, and Weston cringed as two of his four older brothers, Barrett and Alex, passed through his mind. Barrett had dated Connie's sister, Felicity, casually for several years, only to dump her last fall when he got serious with his now-fiancée, Emily Edwards. And although Connie's other sister, Hope, should have known better than to expect a commitment from Alex, she was very hurt when he chose Jessica Winslow over her just before Christmas.

Weston and Connie had never declared their feelings for each other. Theirs had been a tumultuous relationship, sometimes quite hot, with them spending days and days (and nights and nights) together before having a disagreement and "breaking up." A few weeks—or months—would pass and they'd bump into each other again. With their chemistry as scorching as ever, they'd pick up where they left off, and another slew of hot, intense days and nights inevitably followed by a fallout would commence.

If Weston was honest, he'd admit that in the beginning, the roller coaster nature of their time together was a big turn-on. He loved fucking Connie. He loved fighting with her. He loved making up with her. Was it mature? No. Was it hot? Fuck, yes. And he was fairly sure that Connie liked the ups and downs—the excitement of breaking up and making up—just as much as Weston did.

Except, it was getting a little old after a year. He wanted more than fucking and fighting in an endless rotation. He didn't know if it was possible for him and Connie to build something real, but lately he liked the idea of giving it a try. Today he planned to broach the subject with her—to see if she wanted to jump off the carnival ride and give a real relationship a try.

He knew the way Barrett and Alex had treated Felicity and Hope might make it difficult for Connie to trust Weston, but he planned to assure her that he wouldn't treat her as his brothers had treated her sisters. He didn't like the idea that his chance for something real with Connie might be compromised by the actions of his older brothers.

Weston huffed, clasping his jaw in his fingers as the cab neared Connie's apartment. For most of his life, Weston hadn't liked being the youngest of five. So much of his identity was determined by the fact that he was "the youngest English brother," and also by the behavior of the four preceding brothers. Friends and acquaintances somehow expected him to be a younger version of the brother they'd met first: a mini-Barrett, sensible and single-minded like Fitz, a player like Alex, alarmingly smart and awkward like Stratton. Weston was his own person, his own man, and he didn't appreciate it that his personality took a backseat to his brothers'.

Without much input, he'd been told from an early age that he'd grow up to be the legal counsel at English & Sons because, after all, Barrett was the oldest and would take over, and the personalities of his older brothers had determined their positions as well. While Fitz had pursued law for the purposes of compliance, none had taken an interest in the role of legal counsel, so, by default, Weston had been nudged toward law school. Anxious to please—and resigned to a future at English & Sons—Weston had complied. But as the bar exam loomed closer, he had misgivings.

It's not that Weston didn't like the law, he did. He appreciated the logic of it. He loved looking for loopholes or reading briefs with interesting legal arguments. The law itself appealed to him.

But corporate law? Ugh.

What his family didn't know was that Weston had no interest in corporate law, and he dreaded the day he passed the exam because he'd have no more excuses for not working at English & Sons. He'd be consigned there—the youngest English brother falling into line and meeting everyone else's expectations—because that's simply what was anticipated of him.

His brothers and parents would probably be shocked to learn that what Weston really wanted was a job much closer to law *enforcement*. His favorite law school professor was a former employee of the DA's office, and Professor Callum's stories and experiences there were fascinating to Weston— work a man could be proud of. In fact, if he could have any job in the world, he would work for the Philadelphia district attorney's office in the juvenile division.

He knew full and well that turning his back on English & Sons to become a civil servant would not just be *hurtful* to his brothers, whom he loved, respected, and admired, but had the potential of causing a deep rift between them. His brothers had a love for English & Sons that was almost equal to their love for each other. So it raised the question . . . despite the fact that Weston English didn't necessarily enjoy being the youngest English and wanted to strike out on his own, was he ready to betray his brothers? To disappoint their expectations? To hurt them so entirely?

He wasn't.

Just thinking about betraying, disappointing, or hurting his brothers made Weston feel sick. Unfortunately, however, a life of corporate law at English & Sons made him feel trapped and hopeless.

"That'll be six bucks," said the cabbie, and Weston handed the driver a ten, stepping out of the car and slamming the door shut.

Reminding himself that today wasn't about becoming a lawyer or passing the bar or his dubious future at English & Sons, he took a deep breath, thinking of Fitz and Daisy, and fixed a smile on his face. He was genuinely happy for his brother, who was not only getting married today but would be a father in a few short months, too. Weston loved Daisy like a sister, and he was excited to become an uncle this summer. There was plenty of time to wrestle with his future after the wedding. No sense in letting it cast a pall over an otherwise joyful day.

Nodding to the concierge, Weston headed for the elevator, pressing the call button. No doubt Connie would be extra stunning today. With long blonde hair and dark blue eyes, she was the most beautiful girl Weston knew, and again he considered that he'd like for them to try dating—exclusively and without drama.

The elevator opened on the fourth floor, and Weston looked down at the roses and grinned, crossing his fingers that Connie wouldn't be *quite* ready yet, and maybe she'd want to—

"Weston?"

He looked up to find Connie coming out of her apartment, and he instantly smiled at the sound of her voice.

"Con!"

"Um, y-you're early."

For the first time, Weston realized she was wearing jeans, a white T-shirt, and a navy blazer. She had spit-shined brown loafers on her feet and her blonde hair was in a ponytail that trailed smartly over her shoulder in an elegant, uniform wave.

Weston chuckled lightly as he approached. "Not that you don't look gorgeous, but is that what you're wearing? To the wedding?"

"Um . . . I, uh . . ."

Her blue eyes widened, and she flicked a glance downward. He followed it to her hand, which clutched the handle of a rolling suitcase.

Snapping his eyes back up to hers, he searched her face, quickly realizing she looked sheepish and uncertain, maybe a little guilty.

"Are you going somewhere?" Weston asked, gesturing to the suitcase with the bouquet of flowers. When the cellophane rustled, heat flooded into his cheeks, and his breathing hitched. *I'm carrying flowers and she's pulling a suitcase. Something's wrong here.* "You're coming to Fitz's wedding with me today, right?"

Her eyes were sorry, but she averted them quickly and gestured to her apartment door, which was still cracked open. "Wes, come in for a second."

He followed her into the apartment, staring at her suit-case for an extra moment when she leaned it against the wall of her vestibule.

Her apartment was dark and quiet without any of its usual mess. It looked like his apartment when he was planning to leave it for a while.

Connie sat down in a wingback chair in the living room and gestured for him to do the same, but he placed the flowers on her coffee table and put his hands on his hips, standing before her. "What's going on here, Con?"

She took a deep breath and exhaled, reaching into her jacket and pulling out a white envelope with his name on it. "I was going to leave this for you."

"Leave it?" He flicked his glance at the envelope like it contained Anthrax. "What does it say?" She offered it to him, but he shook his head. "You read it."

After a long moment, she muttered, "Fine," pursing her lips, then opening the envelope and pulling out a folded sheet of paper. Her blue eyes searched his face for a moment before she dropped them to the letter, but in that brief moment, he read defensiveness and a little bit of annoyance.

Dear Wes,

There's no easy way to say this.

I've left for Italy. My college boyfriend, Alfredo, lives in Florence and we've decided to give things another chance. I don't imagine I'll be back for a while.

Things just never really happened for us, did they? And yet, I worry that we'll keep running back to each other for the excitement of it. But I don't want to be in a long-term dysfunctional relationship. I'd like to find something better. I want you to find something better, too.

I wanted to tell you sooner and in person, but I kept losing my nerve. Sorry to do this on Fitz's wedding day.

Be happy.
Con

Weston stared at her bowed head for several seconds. He crossed his arms over his chest and tried to take a deep breath, but his chest hurt. "Be happy? Be happy, Con? Be happy that you're dumping me on my brother's wedding day?"

When she looked up, her eyes were sorry, and she spoke gently. "I'm not dumping you. I never promised you anything."

"We've been sleeping together for almost a year."

She shrugged lightly, looking away from him as she refolded the letter. "I wasn't your girlfriend, Wes. We never committed to each other."

That was true. They hadn't.

"Do you love me?" he asked suddenly, instantly regretting it.

He and Connie had never burdened their relationship with feelings. What they had was casual, raw, raging, and fun. Love had never really entered the equation, and he recognized, somewhere deep inside, that it didn't have a place in this conversation. Still, the die was cast and he stood motionless before her, waiting for her response.

"Oh, Wes . . ." She sighed. "Do you love *me*?"

He couldn't form the word *yes*. He couldn't lie like that. Searching her beautiful blue eyes, he clenched his jaw and she gave him a small, sad smile. Sad. It was the first time she'd looked sad since he'd arrived. He'd clocked sorry, guilty, annoyed, and defensive, but not sad until now.

"Con," he started, taking a step toward her as she stood from her chair. "We've never given this a chance, really. I mean, to love each other we'd need to trust each other, choose each other . . . we've never really done that. We sleep with each other for a few weeks, have a big fight, go our separate ways. But, we could—"

"No, we couldn't." She said this simply, without a hint of drama. "The fact is, we like each other, yes. And we're each other's 'sometimes fuck-buddy,' just like my sisters were with your brothers. It's fun while it lasts, but—"

"Con, there's more to us than—"

"No, there isn't. It didn't *happen*, Weston. We've been sleeping together off and on for a year, but we never fell in love with each other. Don't you think it should have happened by now? Organically? Because we felt it?"

"We were doing the casual thing. We could change it up. Be more serious. Stop letting stupid shit get between us."

"No," she said softly, offering him the letter, which he refused. "Roller coasters are fun once a year at an amusement park. But I don't want to ride one all the time, Wes."

He was surprised she felt this way, because he did too. Was it really too late for them? He shook his head, wincing. Despite the way they made him feel, Weston recognized the truth in her words. He'd gotten sick of the back-and-forth nature of their relationship, too. And why hadn't they fallen in love with each other yet? Still, he felt like she wasn't giving them a chance.

"Connie, please . . ."

"You'll thank me one day when you meet the right girl. You'll be grateful not to have to come here with your tail between your legs and tell me it's over. And I'll be grateful that I walked away." She took a deep breath and gave him a brave smile before leaning forward to press her cool lips against his cheek. Her voice was soft and low near his ear. "Don't think I didn't want it, Wes. I wish it had happened for us. It just didn't."

He turned his face toward her, his cheek caressing hers until he met her eyes. She was so close, he'd barely have to move to capture her lips beneath his. "Then, please, Con. Don't go to Italy. Give *me* a chance. Give *us* a real chance."

"No." She swiped at her eyes and shook her head, pulling away from him. "I can't think of anything more pathetic than forcing something that isn't there. But, I'm sorry about the timing. I'm a coward."

"Yes," agreed Weston sourly, "you are."

Her blue eyes glistened as she stared up at him, then she turned and headed back to the door. "It softens the blow, though, doesn't it? That I'm such a cowardly bitch? To leave you high and dry without a date on your brother's wedding day? Makes it easier to be angry, not sad, doesn't it?"

Before she reached the apartment door, Weston reached out for her arm and whipped her around to face him. What he saw in her unguarded eyes surprised him: she'd done this on purpose. She'd already fallen for him. He could see it. Somewhere along the way, she'd fallen in love with him, but he'd missed it. When had it happened? How had he failed to see it? And why hadn't he fallen in love with her, too?

"Con . . ."

A tear trailed down her face as she stared up at him. "What do you feel for me, Wes?"

"I care about you. I like being with you. You're fun and sexy. I feel like you're giving up on this too soon."

Her watery blue eyes stared back into his. "Are you in love with me?"

He sucked his bottom lip between his teeth and dropped his eyes.

"I already knew the answer." She shrugged in a gesture meant to convey apathy, but another tear spilled onto her cheek, betraying her. Her back stiffened as she wiped it away. "And frankly? You're an English brother, Wes, which means I'd be pretty stupid to trust you."

"That's not fair. I'm not Barrett or Alex. I would've given this a real chance."

Connie huffed softly, looking down at her shiny shoes. Weston removed his hand from her arm and reached for her, putting his arms around her waist and pulling her against his chest in the dim hallway. He buried his nose in her hair with a heavy heart. "I'm not ready for this to end yet, Con. I hate you for doing this."

"That's the point," she sobbed softly. "Hate me. Now let me go."

He gulped, loosening his arms, and Connie reached behind him for her suitcase.

"Lock the door when you leave," she said softly, then turned and walked out of her apartment, letting the door close softly behind her.

He thought about running after her. He imagined it. But when he got to the part where she raised her blue eyes to his, waiting for the words she wanted to hear, his brain didn't form them. As much as he liked her, as much as he loved fucking her, as much as it had been an exciting time, and as much as he wished he felt differently . . . she was right. Weston wasn't in love with her. But what bothered him was that maybe, if she'd just given him a chance, he would've gotten there. Instead, based on her sisters' experiences with his brothers, she'd decided to walk away. Par for the course. His older brothers had determined the course of his life yet again. It rankled and bit at Weston, making him transfer all of his anger from Connie to Barrett and Alex.

Looking around her pristine apartment, he grabbed the roses off the table. No matter what choices she'd made today, she didn't deserve to come home to dried, blackened flowers. The red bow, printed with the words "Happy Valentine's Day" in a soft, white script, taunted him as he locked the door of her apartment behind him and threw the flowers into the incinerator.

Happy Valentine's Day?

Yeah, right.

He was going stag to his brother's wedding.

Happy *fucking* Valentine's Day.

Chapter 3

Molly leaned against the bar, downing her second Chardonnay in fifteen minutes. If she'd known a single soul at the wedding besides Daisy, or if she wasn't attending by herself, it would have been easier to relax, but as it was, she was barely hanging on. She'd looked for another familiar face among the guests, but she was pretty sure she was the only friend Daisy had invited from their community theater group.

Not to mention, Dusty had called her twice at home this afternoon. The second time, she'd picked up the phone without putting it to her ear, hung it up, then left it off the hook so he'd get a busy signal if he tried calling again. An hour later, he'd started texting, saying they "needed to talk." Without answering, Molly had deleted the texts and set her iPhone to "Do Not Disturb" so that it wouldn't alert her to any further texts from him. It was bad enough to be stag and entirely alone at a wedding without her jackass of an ex-fiancé making it worse.

Knowing Dusty, he wanted her forgiveness. He wanted to try to smooth things over, because it killed him to be at odds with anyone. Well, screw him. They *were* at odds, and they were going to *stay* that way. He didn't deserve her forgiveness. After all, she was the injured party, wasn't she? She wasn't interested in explanations or apologies or working out anything.

Frankly, at this point, all Molly really wanted was to go home. She was basically just waiting for Fitz and Daisy to finish their photos and arrive at the reception to greet their guests. Once she'd given Daisy a hug and told her what a beautiful wedding it was, Molly would be off the hook. She could slip out of the ballroom of Haverford Park and quietly make her way home, where she would continue drinking until she was as drunk as a skunk, and then she'd pass out and try to forget the day ever happened.

It *had* been a beautiful wedding, that much was true. But, for the first time that Molly could ever remember, she hadn't shed a tear. Not one. Not when Fitz's handsome face clutched at the sight of his beautiful bride walking down the aisle, not when Daisy's father lifted her veil, kissed her cheek, and gave her away. Not when they took their vows, which they wrote themselves and were among the most heartfelt Molly had ever heard. Not when they exchanged rings using the Scottish vows, "With this ring I thee wed, with my body I thee worship, and with all my worldly goods I thee endow," which had leveled her every other time at every other wedding. And as a friend of the bride recited the verses from Corinthians, Molly made her own acidic additions in her head:

> Love is patient and kind . . . *and doesn't knock up the art teacher.*
> Love does not behave rudely . . . *unless you consider it rude to cheat on your fiancée.*
> Love never fails . . . *except when it* totally and completely *fails, leading to the breakup of an engagement.*

As Daisy and Fitz made their joyful walk down the aisle, Molly forced herself to stand and clap half-heartedly from the corner of the back pew, but all she really wanted was to go home. In lieu of home, she decided to hold up the bar. She was so busy feeling sorry for herself, she missed the adorable blond in a tux who sidled up beside her.

"Scotch. Double," he said in a low, terse voice. "Wait. Triple."

Molly shifted only slightly to watch him throw back the lowball glass before wincing in distaste and sliding it back to the bartender.

"Again. Neat."

The old Molly—sweet, gullible, trusting, stupid Molly—from yesterday might have gently laid her hand on his arm and asked him if everything was okay. The dumped, bitter, caustic, on-her-way-to-plastered Molly of today nudged her empty glass forward beside his.

"Another Chardonnay, please?"

"That's three," said the bartender as he filled up Blondie's lowball glass again.

She hooked her thumb at Blondie. "And he's on his fourth, fifth, and sixth, but I didn't notice you counting it out for him."

"It's early yet. Maybe pace yourself, honey."

"If I wanted a lecture, I would've called my dad," she said, shocked to hear the words she was thinking somehow fall out of her mouth.

"Whoa, touchy. Just saying."

"Well, don't," she said softly. "Don't say. Just pour."

As she exchanged words with the bartender, Blondie had stopped with his drink halfway to his lips and was staring at her with his mouth slightly open.

"Hey," he said, his eyes flicking to her breasts for just a second. "You look *almost* as miserable as I feel."

"Imagine how delighted I am to hear that," she answered, putting her back to the bar and looking past him, as though bored.

If she was honest, however, she wasn't bored by him. Maybe, just maybe, for no apparent reason that she cared to explore, her tummy might have filled with butterflies when he locked his blue eyes with hers a moment before.

"Wow." He threw back half the glass of scotch, then low-ered the tumbler to the bar, shifting his body to face her. "Not a big fan of weddings, huh?"

"Not today," she admitted, grasping the stem of her wine-glass after the bartender grudgingly refilled it. The wine was doing its work, making the sharp ache of Dusty's betrayal recede from the front of her mind.

"Amen," he agreed.

"Today, weddings suck."

"Right there with you."

"Love, love, love . . . blah, blah, blah. Whatever."

"Preaching to the choir."

"To have and to hold . . . what does that even mean?"

He wrinkled his nose at her. "I think it just means . . . to have and to hold."

She smirked. "I guess they didn't want to confuse anyone when they came up with that witty line."

His lips quirked up and he brought the glass to his lips again, taking a small sip. "Boy, you're something."

"Am I?" she asked, still channeling acidic boredom, although part of her hoped he wouldn't leave because at least if Blondie was talking to her, she wasn't completely alone. Plus, he was easy on the eyes, it was taking effort not to look at him, and that effort was distracting her from her general misery.

"You're really angry." He leaned a little closer and lowered his voice. "Don't take this the wrong way, but I sort of dig that today."

"What do you dig on the other 364 days?"

He laughed softly, shaking his head back and forth. "Why don't we just worry about today?"

She sighed, taking another big gulp of wine before glanc-ing at him. She shifted her body and fluttered a couple of fingers toward the boutonniere on his lapel.

"Wedding party?"

"Weren't you at the wedding?"

"Back row corner," she said. "I guess I wasn't paying attention."

Fueled by many fermented grapes, she decided to remedy that now. Without even trying to be subtle, she started at his neck then dropped her eyes, inch by inch, to his broad chest, to his tapered waist, to his hips—with strong bets on a toned, chiseled man-V under his sharply creased trousers—to his legs, and back up again. "Friend or family?"

His eyes burned after her blunt perusal. "Family. What about you?"

"Maybe I'm crashing," she deadpanned.

As if dumped schoolteacher Molly McKenna would ever do something as wild as crash a wedding.

He grinned, his eyes a touch darker now as he threw back the rest of his scotch without wincing or gasping. He shoved his glass back toward the bartender, tapping on the rim to indicate he wanted another.

"Really?"

"Crashing," she whispered with a soft laugh of disbelief.

"I've never met a wedding crasher. How did you get in?" he asked, amusement and surprise thick in his voice.

"What?"

"You crashed, right? How did you manage to get in?"

"Oh, I didn't . . ."

Wouldn't that be something? To crash a wedding? To be someone who did something like that? Someone . . . wild?

Either the wine was making her loopy, or the idea of "being wild" for the first time in her life had taken hold of her like a beagle's teeth on a bird's throat. Whatever the reason, it didn't much matter. She looked into Blondie's deep blue eyes, which were twinkling with amusement, and made a quick decision. Licking her lips and lowering her voice to a purr as she'd seen in the movies, she beckoned him closer.

"Want me to tell you? Or show you?"

Shocked by her own boldness, Molly didn't move an inch. She stared at the pulse in his throat, the way it pounded, pushing at the skin forcefully with every throbbing surge of blood. By staring at *his* heartbeat she could ignore the fierce pounding of her own.

"Are you serious?"

Her breathing had suddenly become shallow and quick. Was she? Was she serious? What exactly was she offering? A kiss? Sex? Christ on a cracker, she'd never had sex with anyone but Dusty. Dusty. Her nostrils flared with fury. Dusty who'd cheated on her with Shana. She exhaled raggedly, licking her lips again, emboldened by her fury.

"Try me," she whispered.

He leaned back, his blue eyes almost black as he scanned her body neatly. First her lips, which he stared at with longing, his own tongue darting out quickly before his eyes dropped lower, resting on the swell of her breasts, which she'd purposely shoved into a push-up bra to add a little cleavage to her simple, black, multipurpose cocktail dress. Lower now, he took in her small waist and the gentle swell of her hips, before staring at her feet in black, patent-leather sling backs three inches high with a hot pink heel.

When his eyes returned to hers, they were smoldering. "I like your shoes."

"Thanks," she managed to murmur.

"Let's go."

She gulped soundlessly, her fingers trembling with a mixture of fear and excitement. Half a glass of white wine sat on the bar and she picked it up, tipping it back and swallowing until she'd drunk every drop, holding his eyes all the while.

"Lead the way," she said, in a breathy voice that didn't sound like her at all.

He took the glass out of her hand, then laced his fingers through hers, searching her eyes wildly for an extra moment.

"Don't take this the wrong way . . ."

"What?" she asked, incredibly distracted by the solid warmth of his hand pressed into hers, the way their interlaced fingers fit together.

He shook his head. "You don't seem like the type."

Molly McKenna lifted her chin just a notch.

Just for tonight, she was. Tonight she *was* the type of girl who slept with a stranger at a wedding. Tonight, with someone she'd never see again *after* tonight, she was going to forget she was a responsible, good-girl teacher. Tonight, she wasn't pathetic, jilted Molly McKenna. Tonight, she was going to the wild.

"Tonight," she said, "I am."

"What about the other 364 nights?" he asked, his eyes narrowing slightly, like he was trying to figure her out.

She glanced down at their joined hands, then mustered the courage to smirk.

"Why don't we just worry about tonight?" she suggested.

He tightened his grip on her hand and led her through a side door, out of the ballroom.

Having the reception in his parent's country estate, Haverford Park, where Weston had grown up, was suddenly very convenient. Winding his way through the dimly lit back corridors, from the ballroom, through the dining room, into the service hallway, he made it to the back staircase without running into any other guests, pulling the gorgeous, sexy, intriguing redhead behind him.

With her hair held back with a black velvet hairband, and her conservative cocktail dress adorned, simply, with a single strand of pink pearls, she looked like one of the boring, well-mannered girls he'd grown up with . . . until she'd started speaking to the bartender. He'd been utterly captivated by the sharp whip of her words, the heat of her anger that she tried so hard to conceal with ennui. And then suddenly, when he thought he had her figured out as a single, bitter, antiwedding wedding guest, she pulled out the sexy, informing him that she hadn't been invited to the wedding. She was, in fact, crashing. And she insinuated that she'd gotten in by . . . by . . . by what? Fucking someone? Like one of the valet guys? A waiter? Holy shit, that was hot. It was wicked and oh-so-dirty, but damn, it was hot.

And suddenly it had occurred to Weston in his increasingly soused state: whoever she was? She was perfect. The perfect post-Connie rebound. They'd do the deed, he'd cut the cord with Connie, and he'd move on. Slam, bam, thank you, single, bitter, uninvited wedding guest. Don't mind if I do.

It was certainly preferable to enduring Barrett and Alex's guilty grimaces. The second he'd shown up without Connie, they'd asked where she was, and Weston had made no bones about the fact that his ex-*almost*-girlfriend had shot him down because she didn't want to date an English brother. Even though that was only partially true, Weston was in the mood to pick a fight and felt angry with his older brothers, resentful of being the youngest and subject to the wake of their decisions.

Still pulling the mystery woman up the stairs behind him, he asked, "What's your name?"

"Does it matter?"

"I have to call you something."

"I'm . . . I'm, um . . ."

They got to the first landing and Weston stopped, letting her catch her breath. Moonlight streamed in from a small window whitening her skin, but making the contrast of her red lips and red hair more pronounced. She was ethereal and stunningly beautiful in the soft light.

"Don't think too hard," he teased.

"S-Samaria," she answered, her voice breathless from the run from the ballroom. "My name's Samaria."

Like hell, he thought. "Unusual."

"From the Bible," she said, her breasts swelling with every deep breath she took. Her eyes, which he knew were light brown, appeared deep and dark as they stared up at him, and he couldn't look away, not even if he'd wanted to.

"The Bible?" he murmured.

"Samaria," she whispered, "was a mountainous, central, region of ancient Israel, made notable by the story of the Good Samaritan."

He leaned closer to her. "That's *really* your name?"

Her tongue swept across her lips. "One of them."

"I thought you were lying."

She shook her head. "No. And you?"

Weston swallowed. He didn't want her to know his name. He liked the anonymity between them, and he liked it even more that she'd given him what he guessed was her middle name, not her first. He decided to do the same.

"Stefan."

"Stefan," she whispered, tilting her head to the side and smiling, her white teeth shiny in the moonlight. "Like the king."

He reached out to push a tendril of reddish hair behind her ear, letting his fingers rest tentatively on the soft skin of her face. "The king?"

"From *Sleeping Beauty*," she murmured in a dazed, breathless voice that made his blood rush and his cock twitch.

"Ah," he said, smiling back at her and nodding slowly as he recalled the Disney movie from his childhood. "Yes. That's right."

His smile faded as they stood there on the quiet landing, bathed in the moonlight, holding hands, facing each other. His other hand cupped the apple of her cheek, his palm gently flush against her warm skin as her lovely face tilted up to look at him. Finally, when he could bear it no longer, without asking, without warning, he dipped his head and kissed her.

Molly hadn't been kissed by anyone but Dusty in ten years, which meant that Molly had never been kissed by anyone but Dusty ever. In her whole life.

Until now.

Stefan's lips were firm and soft, and when they touched down on hers, Molly felt an instant rush of adrenaline that made her step forward, closer to the immediate source of excitement and pleasure. He untangled his hand from hers, dropping it to her waist, his fingers rolling and adjusting before spanning her hip and jerking her against his chest.

Molly's eyes fluttered closed as his mouth gently trapped her upper lip, sucking lightly before loosening, only to take it back again. He sighed and she tasted the smoky, woodsy flavor of the scotch he'd been drinking, a smell so foreign and exotic to Molly, it suddenly occurred to her—again—that she was kissing an utter stranger in the moonlit back hallway of someone's house when she was supposed to be at a reception.

For just a moment, she thought she should push against his chest and break off the kiss, withdraw her invitation, turn her back and walk quietly down the stairs. But then what? Even the thought made the heaviness of Dusty's betrayal threaten to overtake her all over again. Thankfully, the touch of Stefan's satin tongue running along the seam of her lips made them open like a flower to sunshine and all coherent thought scattered from her mind like fall leaves swept away by a sudden breeze.

Until now, Molly's hands had been dangling loosely at her sides, but as her lips parted, she raised them to his shoulders and slid them forward until they met behind his neck, where her fingers entwined.

His hand tightened on her face, gently but firmly manipulating her head, tilting it until he had the angle he needed to sweep his tongue into her mouth to meet hers. Molly moaned softly, arching into him as darts of pleasure made her tremble with arousal, with want, with need, with *more* . . . and Stefan met her, stroke for stroke, the velvet heat of his tongue caressing hers as his arm wound around her bowed back to hold her flush against his body.

Through a haze of deep lust, Molly heard the sound of a door opening, and suddenly the staircase was illuminated from below.

Stefan stopped kissing her suddenly, drawing his lips back from hers, his eyes wide and primitive as he searched her face. His body still pushed aggressively into hers, and she felt the evidence of his arousal, probing the place that hid muscles deep inside that twitched and flexed with want.

His breathing was quick and shallow, and his chest crushed her breasts with every draw, making her nipples purse and pebble, pushing back against him with shameful want.

She didn't care.

She didn't care if she was behaving completely out of character.

She didn't care if her actions were reckless and wanton.

She didn't care right now if she'd regret this decision an hour from now.

None of it mattered.

Her body was totally primed for pleasure with this beautiful stranger, and he was the only thing keeping her crushing disappointment and heavy-heartedness at bay. Poised and prepared for more, there was simply no way Molly could turn back now.

"Take me upstairs," she whispered.

"Yeah," he panted softly. "Okay."

His hand drifted over her hip, dropping regretfully, and she loosened her hands from behind his neck. He paused, his palm still pressed intimately against her cheek, his eyes searching her face like she couldn't possibly be real.

"Who are you?" he asked, furrowing his brow. "Really?"

She licked her lips and tilted her neck just slightly so that her mouth slipped under his hand. Letting her eyes flutter closed, she kissed his palm, her tongue slicking a hot path across his skin. When she looked at him, his lips had parted and he swallowed audibly, staring back at her with longing as she whispered,

"It doesn't matter."

Chapter 4

As he pulled her up the rest of the stairs to the third floor of Haverford Park, Weston fought the urge to talk to her, knowing that small talk would be a buzz-kill if the mutual goal here was anonymous sex. Still, he couldn't help the fact that he was interested in finding out more. She dressed conservatively, and despite the forwardness of her words and actions, Weston had a feeling she was somehow out of her comfort zone. *Why? What had happened to her to make her want this, with him, tonight?* (Not that he was complaining.) *Wouldn't it be ironic*, he thought, *if she was using him to take her mind off of someone, just like he was.*

She'd far surpassed his expectations with the kiss they'd just shared. It was unusual for Weston to get completely hard from one kiss—it usually took a little more action than that. But damn if his cock hadn't stood at attention, ready and willing, desperate for the hot, tight feeling of her hidden muscles clenched around him.

Around another corner, and then another, he finally pushed open the back-stairs door that led to the third floor linen room. Through the servant's corridor and out a simple white door, they found themselves at the north end of the family gallery that housed the bedrooms of Weston, his four brothers, his parents, a sitting room, a game room, and two guest bedrooms for close family. The dark wood of the floor and walls glimmered from brass sconces that cast dreamy shadows on the Persian carpet that ran the length of the long hallway.

Without looking back at Samaria—a name he still questioned, despite her handy explanation of its origin—he walked briskly down the hall, past the guest rooms, past the sitting room, past Barrett's room and the grand staircase, stopping at a dark wood door on the other side of the stairs. Her eyes were wide and curious as she looked up at him.

"What?" he asked.

"You really know your way around."

He nodded. "Yeah."

"Are you a brother? Cousin?"

He shrugged. He couldn't help feeling like revealing too much of themselves would ruin the moment and shatter the mystery that propelled them toward anonymous rebound sex in his bed. "Does it matter?"

"Nope," she answered, her lovely face sad.

He looked down at their entwined fingers. He couldn't explain why, but his heart clenched to realize that she was sad. He wondered why. He wondered who or what had made her sad, and had an insane urge to punch something for that brief moment. But when he looked back up, her face was impassive again, all sadness whisked away from her eyes.

He cleared his throat, turning the doorknob. "We can use my—er, um, this room."

"Great," she said, dropping his hand and walking inside.

As opposed to the austerity of the hallway, the room was warm and personal, with pale yellow walls, a large Persian carpet covering the hardwood floor, and a sitting area in front of a fireplace with two comfortable-looking leather chairs. A desk area had been built into one corner and was covered haphazardly with open books and flanked by book cases. In the center of the room, large and slightly intimidating, was a king-sized bed, unmade, with white sheets, three pillows (two unused, one smooshed), and a dark blue comforter hanging half-off the bed.

If she had to guess, Molly would wager it was the room of a college student or maybe a graduate student. It didn't have clothes strewn about or questionable smells wafting up from under the bed, which meant that it was an adult's room, but there was something that felt young about the space, as though it belonged to someone who hadn't totally established himself in the world quite yet.

She took a few steps toward the desk before looking back at Stefan, who'd closed the door and stood motionless in front of it with his hands on his hips. He was tall and handsome, but looked slightly uncertain, which made her smile—a small smile that barely lifted the corners of her mouth—as she meandered toward the desk.

The opened books were law books and other legal texts, including one entitled *Studying for the Pennsylvania Bar*. Squinting in the dim light from a bedside lamp on the opposite side of the room, Molly leaned forward to read the LSAT score pinned to a bulletin board hanging over the desk. The score was from three years ago, and the letter read that Weston S. English had scored a 175 on the test.

"Wow," she murmured.

Stefan crossed the room to see what had captured her attention. "Wow what?"

Molly looked up to find him much closer to her, and she swallowed nervously, gesturing to the bulletin board with her hand. "Whoever Weston English is, he's really smart."

"Why do you think so?" he asked, darting his eyes to the floor.

Was he hiding a smile? She thought she'd glimpsed one before he looked down.

"He scored a 175 on his LSATs," she said. "The highest score is 180. He was almost perfect."

"Almost," said Stefan softly, staring down at his shiny black shoes.

"Do you know him?" asked Molly.

"Yeah."

Molly nodded. Of course he did. They'd already established that Stefan was family. Whether he was Daisy's family or Fitz's family, he'd still know Fitz's youngest brother, Weston English.

She turned her back to Stefan, trying to remember what she knew about Weston, but her mind came up blank. In the short chats she'd had with Daisy backstage, she'd gathered that Barrett English was the oldest of the English brothers and Daisy's fiancé, Fitz, was the second oldest. She didn't know very much about the three youngest brothers, though it occurred to her now that Stefan had very similar coloring to Fitz. Perhaps they were first cousins. She thought about asking him, but the reality was that she didn't really want to know that much about Stefan. Keeping their tryst anonymous was part of the reason she was willing to go through with it at all.

Taking a few short steps to the bed, she sat down on the rumpled white sheets, and stared up at him.

He surprised her by approaching her quickly, wordlessly, and dropping to his knees before her in one smooth move. She gasped, waiting to see what he'd do next, but he reached for her shoe, unbuckling the strap and slipping it off her foot. He did the same to the other, and then ran his palm up the smooth inside of her leg, stopping at her knee, before sliding it back down.

"I think you're beautiful." His eyes were luminous as they looked up at her. "Tell me what you want."

"Take off your jacket," she murmured, as her heart throbbed with excitement and nerves.

Without looking away from her, he shrugged a little and it fell to the ground behind him. Smooth.

"What else?" he asked, his voice raspy and low.

Her breasts heaved against the black scoop neck of her dress, and she summoned all of her courage to ask for what she wanted. Taking a deep breath, she answered him on a breathy exhale.

"Take off the rest."

He blinked at her. Once, twice. Then, with startling speed, he was on his feet, whipping off his tie, pulling at the snaps and buttons of his tuxedo shirt, and yanking his T-shirt off until he stood, bare chested and breathless, in front of her.

Molly stood, staring into his eyes and daring to flatten her hands on the solid, sinewed expanse of his chest. Standing on tiptoes, she tilted her neck, her mouth meeting his with perfect precision. After a surprised moment, his lips kicked into action, kissing her wildly, with abandon, their teeth clashing together as his fingers found the zipper on the back of her dress. He pulled it down with a satisfying *whoosh*, his nimble fingers unhooking her bra as well. Still kissing her, his tongue lapping at hers with urgency, he pushed her dress off her shoulders and it sluiced down her body to land in a heap around her feet.

His arms clamped around her, crushing her bare breasts against the hard muscles of his chest, which twitched under the hard, sensitive skin of her erect nipples. Walking her backward, she felt the mattress against her thighs and fell back with Stefan's body on top of hers. Dipping to accommodate their weight, Molly sighed at the feeling of his hard body pushing down on her softer one, and threaded her fingers through his hair, forcing his mouth to stay with hers. Their tongues tangled and licked, and when he sucked on hers, her already-wet sex flooded slick again. Instinctively, she arched up against his erection, and he slipped his hands under her shoulders to slide her completely onto the bed.

"Damn, this is hot," he murmured, as his lips skated from her lips to her ear, taking the lobe between his teeth as his hand slid down to her breast, molding it with his palm as he rubbed the nipple with his thumb.

Molly gasped and whimpered, pushing her breast into his hand and turning her neck so he had better access to her ear. Her hands wound into his hair, flexing and releasing, and she moaned as he bit her ear again, prompting a low, growly chuckle in the back of his throat. The vibration against her own throat sent goosebumps coursing down her arms, and she slid one leg up the back of his, which, she realized with some surprise and annoyance, still had pants on.

He leaned up on his elbows, kissing and licking his way down her neck until his mouth, hot and wet, hovered over the breast he'd plumped in his palm. Dropping his lips, he took the erect nipple into his mouth and sucked. Molly bucked off the bed, arching into his mouth as tendrils of pain and pleasure unfurled from her chest, teasing her skin and tripping her heart.

Releasing his badly messed hair, she slid her hands down his bare back, only stopping when she reached his waist. Slipping her fingers to the front of his pants, she unbuttoned his pants and pulled at his zipper.

Stefan raised himself and slid back until his feet hit the floor. Molly raised herself on her elbows in time to watch him slip his pants off. He stood in plaid boxers tented in the front by a significant erection. He fell back to the bed, lying beside her on his side, and took her other nipple into his mouth while his fingers traced her lips.

Molly opened her mouth, sucking two digits inside and mimicking the movements of his tongue on her breast, licking, sucking, laving her tongue around his fingers and moaning as the swirling in her stomach made her muscles start to clench in anticipation of—

Knock, knock, knock.

"Wes?"

Stefan jerked his neck up from her breasts, whipping his eyes to the door.

"Shit!" he whispered. Then, a little louder, "One minute."

"Wes, what the hell are you doing? It's time for pictures."

"Jesus, Alex." His voice was breathless. "I said to give me a minute."

Molly stared up at him. His face was turned away from her, but his chest still propelled itself frantically into hers with every panted breath he took.

From the hallway, Molly heard chuckling. "Oh, shit! Wes, are you getting it on with someone in there?"

Stefan—or, more accurately, Wes—finally turned from the door to look down at her face. Pulling his bottom lip between his teeth, he flicked a glance at Molly's swollen lips before finding her eyes again.

"My asshole brother," he whispered, pursing his lips and shaking his head.

"You're Weston English," said Molly, feeling a little dizzy and a lot frustrated. Before Alex's untimely interruption, she was about to have her first—of she hoped many—orgasm. She took a deep, shuddering breath, remaining motionless beneath him as he stared back down at her.

"Weston *Stefan* English."

"I see," she said.

"And you are?"

"Molly McKenna. Molly *Samaria* McKenna. I'm a friend of Daisy's."

His eyes widened and a slow grin spread out across his face. "A friend . . . You're a *guest*. You didn't—"

"Crash?" If it hadn't been so dark, he would've seen her blush. "You don't know me at all, but I'm not really the wedding-crashing type."

"I know you a little more than 'not at all,'" he countered, rubbing his body against hers and leaning down to kiss her again.

Alex rapped on the door, louder this time. "Romper Room! Pictures!"

"God damn it, Alex!" Weston vaulted off of the bed and strode to the door, whipping it open. Molly scrambled to sit up, grasping for a sheet, which she clutched over her breasts. When she looked up at the door, she smiled with relief. Weston had only opened it a crack and was block-ing Alex's view entirely with his body. "What the fuck? I'm occupied. Give it a fucking rest. I'll be down in five minutes."

"Can you finish that fast?" teased Alex, still laughing.

"Fuck you, Alex," answered Weston, slamming the door in his brother's face and locking it before stalking back to the bed.

Leaning down, he picked up Molly's black lace bra and stared at it regretfully for a moment before handing it to her.

"I'm sorry," he said softly, reaching for his pants.

"For what?" she asked, threading her arms through the straps and fastening the bra in the back.

He slipped the pants on and reached down for his T-shirt and her dress. "For not telling you who I was. For my fucking brother. For not getting to finish what we started. Take your pick."

"Don't worry about it."

She took her dress from him and stood to slip it over her head. His hand on her arm stopped her, and she looked up to see him staring at her, his pants and shirt unbuttoned, his eyes hungrily searching her face.

"Molly, I . . . I mean, I . . ." He grinned at her sheepishly, chuckling lightly. "Can I tell you something?"

"Sure," she said, resting her dress over her arm, a little surprised to find she didn't mind standing in front of Weston English wearing nothing but her bra and skimpy underwear.

"There's this girl I've been seeing . . . Connie. She broke things off this morning, and I—" He bit his bottom lip, and his fingers tightened momentarily on her arm.

"Oh," she said, her own broken feelings about Dusty crashing over her like a wave of sadness, a sudden tsunami of grief. Her voice was thready when she said, "I'm sorry."

"It'll be okay," he said, his face falling a little as he shrugged. "Maybe it was for the best. I don't know. But I thought today was going to be horrible." He reached forward to tuck a lock of her hair behind her ear. "Thanks for making it not-so-horrible, Molly Samaria McKenna."

She nodded, clenching her jaw, not trusting herself to speak, their sorrows so very similar.

His fingers trailed down her cheek to rest under her chin as his blue eyes explored her face. His voice was soft, almost dream-like when he murmured, "My very own Good Samarian."

Her chest was tightening and a lump was gathering in her throat. It was sadness for Weston or herself, she wasn't sure, but she certainly wasn't eager to embarrass herself by crying.

"At your service," she said, and he grinned at her, dropping his fingers and turning to pick up his tie.

Working quickly, Molly threw her dress over her head and reached back, struggling to zip it. Gentle hands suddenly rested on her shoulders, turning her around, and she felt his fingers slide down her back, searching for the zipper before pulling it up. Her head bowed, she stared at her bare feet while his hands still hovered near the base of her neck. She closed her eyes as he brushed her hair over her shoulder and dropped warm lips to her skin. The light touch made her breath catch and she trembled with longing, fisting her hands by her sides to keep herself from turning around and reaching for him. The only time today when she'd felt good, felt free of grief, was when she was making out with Weston. It took all of her self-control not to escape into his touch once again.

"Sorry," he whispered near her skin, his warm breath soothing and painful at once.

He let go of her, stepping back as she leaned down to pick up her shoes. She sat on the edge of the bed and slipped them on, buckling them slowly. Finally dressed again, she stood and looked up at Weston, who finished tying his tie and cocked his head to the side, smiling at her. She forced herself to smile back, despite the force of her encroaching melancholy.

"Do I look okay for pictures?" he asked.

She nodded. "Am I okay?"

"Run a hand through your hair," he said gently. "You've got bed-head."

"You too."

He ran a hand through his blond hair before hooking a thumb at the door. "I guess I'll just . . ."

"Yeah," she said, holding on to her plastic smile as the lump in her throat multiplied.

Weston took a step forward and bent his head toward her, dropping his lips to hers and brushing them softly back and forth before pulling away.

"I owe you one, Molly McKenna," he murmured against her lips. Then he chucked her chin gently before stepping away from her.

"Good luck with the pictures," she whispered, watching him turn and cross the room, smiling at her one last time before closing the door behind him.

As soon as the door closed, Molly stopped trying not to cry and sat back down on the bed, letting the tears flow freely. So many confusing and conflicting feelings were battling for her attention.

First, she still felt raw over Dusty, though she realized, with some relief, that she didn't feel sad anymore. Anger had stepped up to the plate pretty quickly this morning after her shower, and grown steadily into her primary emotion as the day progressed. She didn't want to remain angry forever, and she wouldn't, but right now, she was. Angry that he dumped her. Angry that he got someone else pregnant. Angry that she needed to get tested for diseases. Angry that she meant so little to him that he would have treated her like this.

Second, she had to admit that she felt sorry for herself. She was supposed to come to this wedding with her fiancé, and here she was, sitting alone in Weston English's bedroom after a failed attempt to get laid. She felt a little pathetic about that, though the fact that Weston hadn't rejected her buoyed her spirits a little.

Third, in her whole life, Molly had never experienced the chemistry she had with Weston English. Being with Dusty was nothing like the few stolen moments she'd just spent with Weston in the staircase and in his bed. Her nipples still stood erect against the lace of her bra and her panties were soaked. Every inch of skin felt sensitive and turned-on. She moaned softly, realizing that the chances of ever being with Weston again were next-to-none. He hadn't asked for her number or made any indication that he wanted to see her again. It was completely possible that despite the truth, he thought she was a raging slut in light of her behavior.

Whimpering a soft sound of protest, she took a deep breath through her nose and realized that she was surrounded by Weston's scent. Letting herself fall back on the bed, she stared at the ceiling, feeling her racing heart finally begin to calm down. She grabbed his smooshed pillow and held it against her chest, rolling onto her side.

Despite their heat and chemistry, Molly had to admit that part of her—a very real and large part of her that just wasn't being very assertive today—was relieved that she hadn't slept with Weston. Would it have been amazing? Very likely. He was smart, gorgeous, and mischievous, with a body to die for, but if she'd slept with him, she would have felt really, really cheap and dirty right about now. As it was, she wasn't exactly proud of herself for looking like a first-class strumpet. It was no wonder he didn't ask for her number.

"You just got dumped. You don't need anyone asking you out," she muttered. "Now, stop thinking about it."

Sure. Right. Easy peasy.

Stop thinking about the best kisses, the hottest touches, the way she bucked off the bed and almost came from his mouth against her breast. God, what would it feel like to actually have sex with him if she was ready to orgasm through foreplay?

Forcing herself to stop molesting his pillow and sit up took effort, but taking a risk that the door by his desk was a bathroom, she sneaked inside for a moment to freshen up. His words *You've got bed-head* were certainly accurate. Finding a small brush in her party purse, she raked it through her hair, looking at herself in the mirror.

Thanks for making it not-so-horrible, Molly Samaria McKenna . . . My very own Good Samaritan.

It bothered Molly to think that whatever had happened with Weston tonight was the whole beginning, middle, and end of the story. It bothered her that she'd acted so forward and he might think badly of her. It bothered her that they'd both gotten dumped within twenty-four hours, which meant that neither of them was anywhere near ready for someone new. But immediately, it bothered Molly that she still had a wedding reception to attend. Stag. Flicking off the bathroom light, she made her way back down to the festivities.

Chapter 5

Back at the bar forty-five minutes later, Weston found himself scanning the crowd for Molly, and realized that he had—in fact—beelined for the bar after the photos, hoping she'd be there.

"Wes," said Alex, coming up behind him and clapping him on the back. "What're you drinking?"

"Screw you," answered Weston without glancing at his brother.

"Why're you mad at Al?" asked Stratton, suddenly appearing out of nowhere.

"Yeah," said Alex, grinning, daring Weston to admit the reason.

"Hey, Strat," said Weston, turning to face Stratton and leaning his elbows back against the bar. "Question. You're at a wedding. You and Val slip upstairs to your old room. Your shirt's off, her dress is off, you're both having a damn good time. You're about to get it in . . . and Alex knocks on the door."

"What's the question?" asked Stratton.

"How bad do you pound him?"

"Pretty fucking bad," answered Stratton, looking at Alex with disgust.

"Okay, Strat," said Alex personably, winking at Weston. "New question. It's your wedding to Val. She looks gorgeous and the sun's setting and she has her heart set on wedding party photos at sunset with the whole bridal party present. Wes, here, is missing, and Val's starting to get upset . . . on her wedding day. Finally—eureka!—your sweet and attentive brother, Alex, finds Wes getting it on with some random party-goer in an upstairs bedroom. I tell him it's time for pictures, and he tells me to fuck off. Do you want me to cock-block him for Val's pictures or leave him alone to get his rocks off?"

"Cock-block him," said Stratton, without flinching. He ordered two Merlots, and then shifted his glance to Weston. "Sorry, man. It's Val."

Weston rolled his eyes, muttering, "You're such an asshole, Alex," under his breath and turned his back to his older brothers to order a drink.

"You just don't get it yet, Romper Room," said Alex, sliding a lowball glass of scotch toward himself and swirling the ice cubes. "You've never been in love like me and Strat. You're still playing field with cheap pieces of ass like the one you had in your room this—"

He doubt Alex saw it coming.

Weston spun so fast and his fist curled and pulled back with such quick and mighty force, Alex's head had snapped back from the strength of the blow before he was even able to finish his sentence. Stumbling back into Stratton, who grabbed Alex's shoulders to steady him, it took Alex several seconds to regain his bearings.

Weston panted angrily, ready to go again if Alex came at him.

"What the *fuck*?" asked Alex, dabbing at his split lip with the back of his hand.

"Don't talk about her."

"About who? Some chick you picked up to bang at a wedding? Are you seriously—"

The thing about Alex? Sometimes he just didn't think. This time Weston caught his jaw with an uppercut that whipped Alex's head up and back so fast, it slammed into Stratton's forehead.

"Fuck!" exclaimed Stratton, who rubbed his forehead, likely more surprised than injured. "What the hell, Wes?"

"I told him not to talk about her."

"Alex, stop fucking talking about her," advised Stratton, shaking his head at them like they were both crazy before taking his two glasses of Merlot off the bar and turning into the crowd to find Valeria.

"What is *wrong* with you?" asked Alex, rubbing his chin and working his jaw, which was already starting to discolor.

"You don't know her."

"Do *you*?" asked Alex, his eyes furious as he reached for his drink, then winced as the scotch bathed his split lip.

"Better than you do."

"Get yourself together, Romper Room."

"Don't call me that again." He fisted his hands, resting them on the bar.

Alex narrowed his eyes, still massaging his jaw with his thumb and forefinger. "You hit me again, *Weston*, I hit back. Got it?"

Weston nodded.

Alex's tone softened. "I didn't realize she was important to you. I misunderstood the situation."

Weston took another sip of scotch without looking at Alex, curious to find that Alex's word "important" didn't faze Weston in the least. In fact, it felt like the right word, which made no sense at all.

"If you called Jess a 'cheap piece of ass,' you'd be flat on your back by now and you wouldn't come-to for a few hours," he continued. "Sorry about it. I didn't realize there was someone besides Connie."

"It's fine, Alex," said Weston, not bothering to correct his brother.

"I'd like to meet her," he said gently.

"And here I thought your dog days were over," said Jessica Winslow, Alex's fiancée, from behind him. "*Who* do you want to meet? What's her name?"

Alex turned and smiled, hooking an arm around her waist. "Wes's new girl."

Jessica cringed at Alex's face. "What happened to you?"

"My face ran into Weston's fist."

She gave Weston a look. "Do I want to know why?"

"No," Alex and Weston replied in unison.

"Did he deserve it?" she asked.

"Yes," they replied.

"Okay, then," said Jessica, turning to the bartender. "A Bass, please."

Weston grinned, turning away from the bar to look out over the ballroom. Couples filled the dance floor, including Stratton and Val, who looked completely besotted with each other. Here and there people sat at their tables in small groups, chatting or waiting for dinner to be served, while still more people milled around, talking in small groups.

Out of the corner of his eye, Weston caught sight of a redhead in a black dress making her way through the crowd toward Daisy and Fitz, and suddenly his feet couldn't move fast enough.

"Thank you so much for inviting me today," said Molly, holding Daisy's hands after giving her a careful hug and kiss.

"You aren't leaving, are you?"

"I-I think I am," said Molly, cringing a little.

Out of nowhere, Weston suddenly appeared at Daisy's side, smiling a five thousand kilowatt smile in Molly's direction.

"Hi, again," he said.

Molly's stomach fluttered and her heart skipped a beat. It was the first time she'd seen him in full light—not the dim light of the bar, the moonlight on the stairs, or the soft bedside light of his bedroom—and he was so beautiful, her breath caught. He looked like Alex Pettyfer on a bad day. He looked delicious.

"H-Hi," she managed, chuckling softly for no reason as her cheeks flushed with warmth.

Daisy squeezed her hands. "Can I meet Dusty before you go? I've heard so much about him."

Molly's eyes cut to her friend's, her mouth opening in dismay. "Oh. Oh, um, I . . . well, he couldn't make it."

"What? Oh, no! Is he all right? Is everything okay?"

Daisy searched Molly's face before furrowing her brows together delicately. Dropping her eyes to their joined hands, she gently turned over Molly's left hand, sucking in a quiet breath to find the fourth finger empty. "Oh, Molly."

Molly pulled her hands away, licking her lips nervously and darting a quick glance to Weston, who watched the interaction with interest and confusion, and finally . . . compassion.

"It's fine," she said lightly, forcing herself to smile. "Some things aren't meant to be. Unlike you and Fitz, who look so happy today."

Fitz drew his wife against his side, kissing the coiled braids on her head tenderly, but Daisy's sympathetic eyes still reached out to Molly.

"I'm sorry, Molly."

"Oh, no, please," she said, horrified to feel her eyes watering. "It's your day. The happiest day. That's all that matters."

"Hey, *Molly* . . . Are we still on for that drink before you go?"

Molly gratefully turned her head to look at Weston, who wore an easy smile. Deceptively easy, because behind it, Molly read empathy and kindness. He knew she was about to cry. He could see it, or somehow sense it, and he offered her an escape.

"Yes," she answered, blinking. She turned back to Daisy, offering the best smile she could. "You're so beautiful, Daisy. Congratulations."

Grateful for Weston's hand under her elbow, while incredibly humiliated by the way he just found out she'd been dumped by her fiancé, she couldn't bear to look at him as he steered them out of the ballroom once again. An hour ago, he'd led her upstairs with sparks leaping between them. This time, he was less hurried, more gentle, and sparks? Well, it's hard to make sparks when you're about to turn on the waterworks.

"I know where your room is. I'll just go sit by myself for a minute and get myself together," whispered Molly as they climbed up the stairs. "You don't have to come with me."

"Yeah, I do." He ran his hand down her forearm until he found her fingers and laced his with hers. "Why didn't you tell me?"

"Tell you what?" she sobbed softly. "That my fiancé called me last night to say he wasn't coming to Philly? That he knocked up the art teacher while we were apart? That he broke off our engagement? Should I have told you that before you took off my dress or after?"

"Molly," he said gently, stopping on the first floor landing again and tipping up her chin with his finger. "I'm sorry."

She didn't meet his eyes. "Please don't. Please don't feel sorry for me. It'll make me cry ten times harder."

He didn't say anything else. As he put his arms around her and pulled her against his chest, Molly caught a glimpse of his watch: 7:06 pm. And Molly, who'd had no one to lean on for twenty-four long, miserable hours, placed her damp cheek on Weston English's shoulder and decided to lean on him.

As Weston processed what had happened to Molly, a fierce anger rolled around in his gut, and for the third time in one night, he wanted to punch something.

Suddenly all of her behavior made sense: her bitterness over weddings, the way she kept downing glasses of wine, how untypically—he sensed—forward she'd been. She'd been dumped last night and not by her on-again, off-again boyfriend, but by her fiancé, the man who was supposed to recognize how goddamn lucky he was to be making her his wife.

Wait. What?

He shook his head mentally, erasing that last thought like the back of a pencil to paper.

Her small body curled into his, her shoulders shaking lightly from tears as she rested her weary head on his shoulder, and Weston felt profoundly protective of her. He knew in his bones that she wasn't easy and she wasn't loose. She was heartbroken.

"I'm not going to say I'm sorry for you. But, I do think your ex is a douchebag."

Her shoulders shuddered again, but he heard the small sound of sob-filled laughter escape from her throat, and he smiled to himself, wondering how to make it happen again.

"I mean, I'm speaking from experience here, and this guy is a monumental jackass."

She sniffed softly and giggled again. "Experience?"

"Absolutely. He gives up a girl who kisses like you do? He's a douchebag, a jackass, *and* certifiable. Completely insane."

"We never kissed like that," she said quietly.

"What do you mean?" he asked, adjusting his hands on her back, remembering the satin feel of her skin beneath.

"Dusty and I never kissed like that." She swallowed before continuing in a soft, breathless voice. "I've never kissed *anyone* the way I kissed you. I've never felt like . . ."

Weston tried to take a deep breath, but it took more concentration than he expected and sounded more ragged than it should have. "Felt like what?"

"Like . . . like thunder and lightning," she said.

His breath hitched from her words, and her fingers, which had been trapped flat against his chest between them, flexed and bent slightly before flattening again. That little movement was all it took for the pulse in his throat to jump.

"What was it like with him?"

Molly took a deep breath, presumably trying to come up with the words to describe what it was like kissing her douchebag, jackass, certifiable ex.

"I don't know," she finally whispered. "Fine, I guess. Okay."

"What about the other guys you've kissed?" asked Weston. "Were they like thunder and lightning? Or just okay?"

"What other guys?"

"You know . . . in high school." He shrugged. "Or college."

"Oh, um, they, um, they were . . . fine, too."

"So, I'm the only storm," he joked.

"Right now? You're the eye of it, Weston," she said softly, readjusting her cheek against his shoulder, letting her body rest limp against his. "You're the calm."

He listened to her breathe, the way her breaths became deeper and more relaxed the longer he held her. He stopped feeling the weight of her cheek on his shoulder, almost as if her weight was part of his body and always had been. Her breasts, which had hardened for him before, remained plush and pliant against his chest, but her softness moved him. How had he missed this when he first saw her? The gentle womanliness of her. With the moonlight streaming in over her shoulders, her hair glowed red, making the whole snow-covered world of Haverford Park pink outside the window. It was like looking through rose-colored glasses, but he was looking through Molly instead.

"You're not crying anymore, Molly," he said gently, loosening his arms from around her.

She lifted her head and stepped back, swiping at her eyes, and pressing her palms against her flushed cheeks.

"But you're still sad," he observed.

"Not as much as I was."

He grinned. "Hey . . . remember before? How I said that you helped make this not the most horrible wedding ever?"

She nodded, chuckling lightly at his awkward wording.

"Well . . . what would make it less horrible for *you*? More drinks? Dancing? Dinner? Cake? I can go steal some cake for you."

Molly giggled softly, dropping her hands from her face and smoothing her dress. "I can't let you steal Daisy's cake."

"No, I guess you couldn't. Plus, I've already had an altercation with one brother tonight. I'd prefer to avoid one with the groom."

"You're sweet," said Molly. "But I think I'll just go home."

"Not allowed," said Weston. "I can't let you go home and be all sad and alone. We both got dumped, right?"

She nodded.

"We're a perfect pair, Molly McKenna. I literally can't stand anyone's company tonight but yours. What will it take to get you to stay?"

It felt like a major triumph when her lips tilted up just a little. "I don't know . . ."

Suddenly Weston had an idea. The best idea. The best place in the world. The place that always cheered him up when he was feeling down. "I've got it!"

"Got what?"

"Come with me. If this place doesn't cheer you up even a little, you can go home, okay? Deal?"

Her little grin widened just a little as she stared up at him, and his heart clutched from the tentative hope that flitted across her face.

"Deal."

Chapter 6

Molly had no idea where they were headed, but Weston took her hand in his, weaving their fingers together like they'd never been apart, and turned them back down the stairs. His excitement was infectious, though, and Molly found herself smiling as he burst through the downstairs door, steering her through a dark hallway before coming out in the kitchen. Offering hellos to the twenty-odd people pulling together the hors d'oeuvres and wedding dinner, he crossed the large expanse of white-tiled floor and headed out through a doorway in the far corner that led to a cobblestoned mudroom.

The walls were painted a cheerful robin's egg blue and coats hung on hooks to Molly's right while bright white cubbies under a long bench held boots of all sizes to the left.

Weston dropped her hand to push through the coats and jackets, finally finding a bright red canvas barn jacket with a quilted, flannel inside and a smart brown leather collar. He held it out to her. "This is my Mom's."

She took it from him, searching his eyes.

"Nope. I'm not telling you yet. Just put it on."

He'd tidily read her mind, and she grinned, shrugging into the jacket and appreciating its warmth in the drafty room while he took a similar jacket in dark blue and traded it for his tux jacket. Taking her hand, he led her to the bench on the other side of the room and gestured for her to sit. Kneeling down in front of her for the second time tonight, he unbuckled her heels, taking them off gently and putting them beside her on the bench.

"I love these shoes," he said softly, looking at her from the floor with an adorable grin.

"I remember."

"They're hot," he said, a lock of blond hair falling over his forehead rakishly as he caressed her ankle. "Like the girl wearing them."

"You're good for my ego." She sighed.

He chuckled softly, placing her shoes to the side and handing her a pair of red and navy Wellington boots.

"Your Mom's?" she asked.

"See if they fit."

She slipped them on and they were a little snug, but not enough to complain. She looked back at him and smiled.

"Now will you tell me where we're going?"

"Nope."

He dispatched his own shoes, trading them for some snow boots trimmed in cream shearling, then offered Molly his hand again, which she took, giggling quietly like they were up to no good.

He led her outside, and she gasped, surprised by the bite of the cold on her bare legs.

"Damn. I should've pilfered mittens and a hat, too," he said, squeezing her hand. "You too cold?"

"It's freezing out!" she said, watching her breath float up to the star-covered sky.

"It's not far. Trust me?" he asked, grinning.

"Yeah," she said, smiling back, surprised that the word slipped from her lips so easily.

"Then come on!"

He tugged on her hand and they walked briskly through a parking area filled with party rental vans and flower delivery trucks, then continued around the back of a garage, their booted feet crunching cheerfully on the ice-covered flagstones.

They turned another corner and that's when Molly smelled it: fresh-cut hay. In the middle of February. Like a miracle.

She stopped in her tracks. "Oh, I love that smell!"

"You do?"

"More than any other." She sighed, pulling her bottom lip between her teeth as she smiled up at him.

"Then you're in luck," he said, grinning with delight. Opening the back door of a long, stone building, he stepped inside and Molly followed.

It was pitch black, but Molly closed her eyes and breathed deeply. Home. It smelled like home, and her eyes welled tears of surprise and gratitude. Hay, horses, leather, hard wood. The combination of smells was more comforting and familiar—beloved, even—than Weston could have possibly guessed.

"Molly?" he asked.

Her eyes fluttered open to find him staring at her. He'd flicked on a desk light by the door and now she realized they stood in the tack room of a stable. Before her, ten or more different saddles hung from hooks on a wall with bits and halters hanging below. At the top of the wall, along the ceiling, shiny horseshoes were nailed into place, and the blond wood floor was clean and shiny.

"Christ on a cracker," she murmured, breathing deeply again. "This is the prettiest tack room I've ever seen."

Stepping further into the room, she noticed the dark green trunks on the floor, lined up to make a long bench, each with diamond shaped initials monogramed on the center. Finding <WES>, she sat down gingerly, looking at the neatly stacked velvet riding caps on the counter in front of her.

"Your initials spell your nickname," she said softly, brushing her palm over the gold letters behind her legs.

"Yes, they do."

She smiled before looking behind his shoulder at a large, framed photograph of five boys sitting atop five horses.

"Is that you and your brothers?"

"Uh-huh." He turned to look at the photo, pointing to the smallest child. "Me."

"I'm the youngest too," she said, suddenly missing her family so much it ached.

"Of how many?" he asked, putting his hands in his pockets and leaning against the counter.

"Four. My sister, Claire, is three years older than me. My twin brothers, Travis and Todd, are five years older."

"Tough being the youngest," he said.

"Oh, I didn't mind," she answered, standing to check out the saddles. "I love being the little sister."

"We don't have that in common."

"You don't love being the little sister?" she teased.

He chuckled softly from his place against the counter. "Touché."

"These are beautiful saddles," she said, running her fingertips over the shiny leather of a smaller-sized western that would suit her. It was so supple and pretty, she wondered if it had ever been used. "Someone takes really good care of them."

"Why do I get the feeling you're 100 percent at home in a tack room?"

"Because I am," she admitted. "Though not one this fancy. Or big. Or clean." She giggled softly, turning around to look at him.

"You like horses?" he asked, his face younger and more innocent in the soft light of the tack room. He'd chosen this place to cheer her up, and she realized that she hadn't seen him so happy and relaxed since she met him. He was totally at home here in the stable, and she paused in her thoughts just for a moment to appreciate they had that in common.

"I love them. We have four back at home."

"Where's that?"

"Hopeview, Ohio."

"You grew up on a farm," he said softly. A statement. A realization.

She grinned. "I did. A little farm in the middle of Ohio."

"Dairy?"

"No. Corn, wheat, soybeans, and cotton."

"I wonder what that was like," he said, taking a step closer to her.

"Honestly?"

"Yeah, honestly."

"Loving. Warm. Hard work. Early mornings. Early nights." She shrugged, another wave of homesickness threatening her lighter mood. "Home."

"And you miss it," he said, coming to stand beside her.

Molly's body was still angled toward the saddles, but now she shifted slightly and faced Weston. "Not usually. I really do love Philadelphia. I love my work. But . . ."

"You gave up a lot to move here, right?"

"More than I knew at the time," she whispered, the meaning behind his words not lost on her. "I'm not homesick, though. I'm really not. But I think, when bad things happen, sometimes you just want to go home."

Weston's heart swelled as he stared at sad eyes in her pretty face. He barely knew her, and yet he couldn't stand for her to look sad when he knew the bright sunshine of her smile.

He opened his arms to her, holding his breath as she looked at him before stepping forward into his embrace. Once she was tucked safely against his body, he exhaled, resting his chin on top of her head.

"Don't," he whispered. "Don't go home. Not yet."

"Are you talking about tonight?" she murmured, her breath warm and soft against his throat.

"I don't know. Don't go home to Ohio. Don't go home to . . . wherever home is here. Don't go anywhere," he beseeched her softly. "Just stay here with me for a little while."

She sighed, and he felt the tension leave her body. He backed them up until he hit the counter behind him. He leaned back on it, and she leaned into him.

"Can I ask you something?" she said after a few peaceful minutes.

"Sure."

Apparently they were going to have a conversation with his arms around her and her body nestled snugly into his. Fine with Weston. As long as he got to hold her, he'd talk as long as she wanted to.

"Why do you hate being the youngest?"

He took a deep breath and his chest swelled into her breasts. Even with their coats between them, it distracted him terribly. "I don't know."

"Yeah, you do," she said, encircling his waist with her arms.

She was hugging him. For whatever unknown reason, it filled him with tenderness that she was holding onto him too. It was as though she sensed the deeply fraught nature of her question and wanted to offer him comfort. It made him want to answer her truthfully.

"It's like . . . well, like this . . . think of the English brothers as a field. A blank field. Brown earth. No plantings."

"Fallow."

He chuckled lightly. "Fallow, says the farmer's daughter. Yes. Fallow."

"And . . ." she prompted.

His hands were flat on her lower back, but his fingers moved now, idly, gently, against the rough canvas of the jacket she wore, frustrated by the barrier.

"And Barrett goes first into the field, making nice, sharp, neat, even rows. And then Fitz joins him. His rows are even neater and sharper, and he also carefully plants seeds in his rows. Suddenly Alex comes along and races around through the field messing up the rows and cackling with glee. So, Barrett puts him in a headlock while Fitz straightens out the rows, and Stratton shows up to build an irrigation system so that Fitz doesn't have to water the seeds every night. And then Weston's born." He cleared his throat, feeling a little silly. "Does that make any sense?"

"Yes," she said. "I see."

"Do you? Because I feel like that was the worst analogy ever."

"No," she reassured him, her hands stroking his back. "I get it. The field could've been anything, but by the time you got there, there were rows and seeds and plantings and zig-zag footprints and irrigation systems. So, where's your piece of the land?"

"Exactly." He sighed, leaning away to look down at her eyes with wonder. She blinked up at him in surprise, light brown eyes almost amber. "I think you're amazing."

She shrugged lightly, shaking her head with a small smile on her face. "Nah. I just understand . . . being the youngest too."

He reached up and put his hand on the back of her soft reddish hair, easing her face against his chest and loving it when she turned her neck so her cheek rested there.

"I don't want to be a corporate lawyer at English & Sons," he suddenly blurted out.

Because he'd never said the words out loud before, he gasped lightly after hearing them drop from his lips. He hadn't actually meant to say them, only think them, but his heart raced and his breath caught—they were out there now. The words. The truth. Only Molly and the saddles had been witness, but it was too late to take them back now.

"So, do something else," suggested Molly gently.

"It's not that simple," Weston protested, suddenly feeling uncomfortable. He didn't want to discuss what couldn't be. He wasn't ready to let down his brothers, to let down his parents, and disappoint them all by turning his back on their life's work.

He loosened his hands from her back and stepped away from her.

Molly searched his eyes in confusion, but he didn't know what to say. Part of him wanted to tell her everything, wanted to hear her sweet voice tell him that he was strong enough to make his own way in the world, that his brothers wouldn't hate him forever, that his destiny was in his hands and no one else's. But she barely knew him. It wasn't her job to sort out his life for him.

"Weston," she whispered, tilting her head back to look up him. "Kiss me instead."

Whatever surprise he felt at her request was knocked out of play by the words *Kiss me*.

He didn't think.

He grabbed her around the waist, yanking her against his body roughly as his lips landed flush upon hers.

God damn.

She was right.

Thunder and lightning.

He didn't tease her as he had on the stairwell when they first kissed. His tongue plunged into her mouth and she tangled with it, sucking on it, her hands sliding up his back into his hair and fisting. The sucking and pulling hurt and felt good and felt hot, and he welcomed it, hating the layers of clothes between them.

He had a quick mental flashback to Molly lying on his bed, her nipple in his mouth, her body tensing and tightening beneath him. He groaned, hardening everywhere almost instantly, wondering what her face would have looked like thirty seconds later if Alex hadn't interrupted them. His fingers curled into fists against her lower back, his short nails digging into the red canvas as he plundered her mouth with his tongue, tasting her, exploring her, discovering the hot, wet heaven that was Molly McKenna's mouth beneath his.

A small whimper from the back of her throat clued him into the fact that he was holding her very tightly, almost aggressively, and worried he was hurting her, he dragged his lips away from hers. Bending forward to rest his forehead on hers, his breathing was ragged and shallow and impossible to catch.

She leaned limp and breathless against him, her clipped breaths loud in his ears. Her fingers relaxed, and she lowered them from his hair, but laced them around his neck, laying her cheek against his chest as she had before, so close to his heart, he imagined she could hear it roaring beneath her ear.

"Instead of what?" he panted, needing a distraction, half-mad with lust for her.

"What?" she gasped softly, out of breath.

Was her heart hammering as hard and fast as his? What was happening between them? And how was it happening so goddamned fast?

"You said, 'Kiss me *instead*.'"

"Oh. Mm-hm. Instead of trying to figure it all out tonight," she answered, sliding her hands to his face and drawing him back down for another kiss.

Hers was an infinitely gentler kiss than his, her small, cold fingers softly curling into the skin of his cheek as she licked and sucked on his lips. Her pace was unhurried, as though exploring him, so different from his wild rush to possess her a moment before, but it reassured him that he hadn't hurt or frightened her. She wanted more of him just as he wanted more of her. His hands on her lower back relaxed, and he laced them together, holding her tenderly as she calmed him with her softness.

Once thing was certain: her fiancé was the stupidest man ever born, because this girl—this beautiful woman in his arms—was spectacular. Any man who had a chance with her would have to be—

Buzz. Buzzbuzz. Buzz. Buzzbuzz.

"You're buzzing," Molly murmured against his lips.

"Ignore it," he said, his voice—drunk with passion—almost unrecognizable in his ears as his tongue flicked softly over her lips, answering her gentle touch with his.

Buzz. Buzzbuzz.

"Answer it," she whispered, drawing back from him.

Her eyes were very dark and wide, her lips red and kiss-swollen.

"Molly, Molly, Molly," he murmured, leaning forward to nuzzle her nose with his, his chest heaving into hers with unrequited longing. "I don't want to."

Buzz. Buzzbuzz.

She lowered her hands and pushed against his chest. Not hard, but hard enough to get his attention. "Answer it, Weston. It could be important."

Regretfully, he unlaced his fingers and reached into his pocket. Seeing Barrett's name on the screen almost made him throw the phone across the room. He swiped the screen with frustration.

"*What?*"

Barrett's voice was clear despite the loud hum of the party behind him. "Ten minutes to toasts. Where are you?"

Weston flinched, looking at Molly, who wore an inquisitive look on her face. His lips tilted up in a smile. *God, she's adorable . . .*

"I'll be there." He pressed end and tucked the phone back in his pocket without ever dropping her eyes. "Toasts."

"Ah."

"I, uh . . . I didn't get to introduce you to the horses."

"We'll just have to come back," she teased.

Relief filled his body like sustenance. He hadn't realized how sad it would make him to have to say good-bye to her until this moment. "You're not leaving yet?"

"And miss your speech? No way."

"You're staying," he said, hearing the pleased wonder in his own voice.

"For a little longer," she said.

He grinned. "I promise we'll come back later."

"I'll hold you to it."

Then she took his hand, lacing her fingers through his and pulling him toward the tack room door.

Chapter 7

After they'd hung up the coats and changed back into their party shoes, Weston led Molly back through the kitchen to the closest powder room, kissing her gently before promising to come find her later.

"Promise you won't leave?" he asked.

"I promise."

"I'm going to be looking for your face in the crowd, Molly McKenna."

"Then I'll be sure you can see me," she replied, leaning up on tiptoes to press her lips to his again.

He shook his head, smiling at her, then drew back, running down the hallway toward the ballroom as Molly entered the powder room. She realized that she'd left her purse upstairs on the counter in Weston's bathroom, but she didn't want to be late for his toast, so she dragged her fingers through her hair, grateful she'd opted for L'Oréal Infallible, because she'd done enough kissing tonight to wear off any normal lipstick.

Kissing.

She'd lost track, at this point, of how many times she'd kissed Weston. On the stairs, in his bed, in the tack room . . . he'd kissed her tentatively and softly on the stairs, with more hunger in his bed, but the tack room kiss had blown her mind. Starved, eager, demanding, and fierce, it felt almost savage in its raw lust.

Thunder and lightning? That barely seemed to strike at the surface now. They were like flint and stone. Gunpowder and a match. She'd never felt anything like it in her whole life. But what did it mean?

She was just getting out of an engagement that ended in betrayal and pain, and Weston had shared that the girl he'd been seeing had broken things off this morning. Neither was remotely in the right place for a new relationship. And yet ever since Weston had rescued her from crying all over Daisy's wedding dress, she'd felt a subtle shift between them from random hook-up to something more. Was that crazy?

"A little," she whispered to her reflection. But it was the truth, too. And she couldn't account for it, but she didn't care to explore it any more than she already had.

While she was with Weston in the tack room, she'd barely thought about Dusty once, and the crushing weight of his betrayal had been kept at bay through Weston's hugs and kisses. The timing was all wrong for Weston to be anything but a wedding-fling, but Molly found she was satisfied with that, and just for tonight, she was going to try to enjoy the ride.

Exiting the bathroom, she walked down a long corridor, past several doors and anterooms, by the sweeping front staircase, through a small parlor, and back into the grand ballroom. *My God*, she thought, taking a sweeping view of the room. Even though she'd leaned against the bar and drunk several Chardonnays in this room less than two hours before, she hadn't processed the full scope of the space. *My parents' entire house could fit into this room.*

Plucking her name card from the leftovers on the table just inside the door, she looked around the buzzing room for table eleven, finally locating it on the far left side of the ballroom. Stopping for another glass of Chardonnay first, she joined the other guests who were looking for their seats.

At the front of the ballroom, there was a raised stage with a six-piece band that was playing a slow, sweet melody, and Molly recognized it as "Would You?" from *Singin' in the Rain* and grinned to herself. It was her mother's favorite movie, and she'd easily seen it over twenty times in her life. Humming softly as she made her way through the crowd to her table, she remembered the words:

> *He'll kiss her with a sigh.*
> *Would you? Would you?*
> *And if the girl were I*
> *Would you? Would you?*

"I wish I was the man who put that smile on your face," said a low, sexy, French-accented voice from beside her.

Molly looked up, flustered but flattered to find a very handsome, dark-haired man to her left.

He winked. "Make my day and tell me you're at Table Eleven?"

She grinned at his charms, holding up her card. "Done."

Laying one hand over his heart, he offered her the other. "Rousseau. J.C. Rousseau."

"Molly McKenna," she answered, chuckling softly. She guessed he was several years older than she, infinitely more sophisticated and brutally handsome.

"Molly McKenna," he said, looking into her eyes and holding onto her hand. "The pleasure is all mine."

She laughed a little sound of nervousness and pulled her hand away. He took the liberty of putting his hand flat on the small of her back and led her the last few feet to the table. There were two seats left, and J.C. pulled out one, gesturing for her to sit. Molly sat down, casting a quick look around the table.

"Everyone? This is Molly. *Charmante* Molly."

Eight sets of eyes looked at Molly in unison, and she felt her cheeks flush to be the object of so much attention.

"Hi, Molly," said the woman to her left. "I'm Jacqueline Rousseau. J.C.'s sister."

"But everyone calls her Jax," said the stunning woman sitting beside Jax. "And I'm Madeline Rousseau, but everyone calls me Mad."

"Jax and Mad," repeated Molly, offering them both a friendly smile, while puzzling internally about such odd nicknames.

"I don't suppose you know the Winslows?" asked J.C., bending down to whisper intimately in her ear.

"N-No."

J.C. pointed to the insanely handsome quartet of brothers sitting across from her. "Brooks, Preston, Christopher, and Cameron."

Four sets of perfect teeth flashed swoon-worthy smiles, and Molly waved at them weakly. "Hi."

"And next to Cameron is Margaret Story."

Margaret, who was waiting to return to her conversation with Cameron Winslow, turned to say a quick hello to Molly.

"And finally we have Margaret's lovely sister, Betsy—" The woman to J.C.'s immediate right gave him a warning look and he laughed softly. "*Elizabeth* Story."

Elizabeth winked at Molly. "He's a terrible flirt. Just ignore him. We all do."

Molly grinned and nodded as J.C. pretended to be hurt.

"Are you all related?" Molly asked.

"No, no," said J.C., finally sitting down beside her and leaning so close she could smell the sweet champagne on his breath. "Mad and Jax are my sisters." His face clouded over momentarily and his voice lost its playfulness. "My, um, my little brother, Ten, uh, Étienne, wasn't able to be here tonight."

"Is he all right?"

"I hope so," said J.C. "I mean, I think so. He *has* to be."

"I'm sorry," she said, wondering what was wrong with Étienne Rousseau, but hesitant to pry.

"He got some bad news, and . . ." J.C. fingered the rim of his lowball glass distractedly. "I'm afraid he was in a very bad accident."

"Oh, no!"

J.C. nodded, allowing his concern to be masked quickly by a tight smile. "But, he has good care, and this . . . this is a wedding. We won't dwell on the sad things. To answer your question . . . No, we're not all related, *mignon*. But we all grew up together. On this street, in fact."

"You grew up with the English brothers!" Molly exclaimed.

The music ended and Molly looked away from J.C. to see Barrett English take the stage. The bandleader stepped forward with a microphone, adjusting it to Barrett's height, and Barrett began speaking about his brother, Fitz, and Daisy.

"I did indeed," said J.C., whispering close to her ear, his deep voice warm and teasing. "May I ask which of them got his hooks into you?"

Molly's eyes cut from the stage to J.C.'s fathomless brown eyes. "You're forward."

"I'm charming," he countered.

"Yes, you are." She grinned like he was incorrigible. "I suspect it lets you get away with a lot."

He put his arm around the back of her chair. "We'll see, *mignon*."

The room exploded into applause for Barrett's toast, and Molly felt a little bad that she'd missed it, since Barrett looked like someone who had very meaningful things to say. Alex English stepped up to the mic next and introduced himself with an off-color joke. J.C. Rousseau laughed beside her, the low rumble pleasing.

"Do you know Alex?" J.C. asked her.

"Everyone knows Alex," whispered Jax, to her left.

"Not me," said Molly, smiling politely at J.C.'s younger sister.

"And not you," growled J.C. at Jax, with a direct look.

"Shut up, J.C.," said one of the Winslow brothers from across the table. "He's reformed."

"Alex? Never."

The Winslow brother seated next to the older Story sister—Molly believed his name was Cameron—looked like steam was about to come out of his ears. "Shut it, Rousseau. *Ferme la* douche, huh?"

J.C. chuckled softly beside her, not the least bit bothered by the Winslows' hot-headed warnings.

The crowd clapped again for Alex, and two of the Winslows hooted loudly and clanked their champagne flutes together as he exited the stage.

"And next is Stratton," said J.C. with a smirk. "This should be amusing."

"Why?" asked Molly.

"Stratton has a certain *je ne sais quoi*. He is . . . unique. Especially at social events," said J.C. with a hint of mockery as his fingers gently stroked her shoulder.

Molly leaned forward to grasp the stem of her Chardonnay glass and took a long sip. When she sat back, his arm was still draped across her chair, but he kept his fingers to himself.

Stratton's speech was lovely, and Molly—in addition to every other woman in the room—nearly swooned when he read a love letter from Robert Browning to Elizabeth Barrett Browning that included the phrase "Words can never tell you, however—form them, transform them anyway—how perfectly dear you are to me—perfectly dear to my he and soul."

"My, how he's improved," commented Jax, licking her lips.

"He's taken, *cherie*," Mad whispered to her sister. "Very taken. Very recent."

"Our loss," said Jax, air toasting her sister regretfully as she sipped from her champagne flute.

As Stratton exited the stage, Molly sat up straighter, shifting in her chair a little so she faced the stage, not the table. It was Weston's turn, and she meant to hang on every single word.

"Ah-ha," said J.C., giving her a sly look. "Weston. Now I see, *mignon*."

Molly grinned, pressing her index finger against her lips, and as he nodded, she turned her gaze to the stage.

Weston's eyes scanned the audience for Molly as he made his way onto the stage. He'd casually asked Daisy where she was seated and with a knowing grin, Daisy had shared that Molly was at Table Eleven with the Winslows, Rousseaus, and two of the Story sisters. Weston had to admit, his heart had fallen at this news. Not that he couldn't hold his own, but Daisy had sat Molly at a table with five eligible men, and there was no possible chance they were going to somehow miss how sweet and beautiful she was.

Finally locating her, however, he was somewhat mollified to see that she was sitting next to Jax Rousseau, who was two years younger than Weston and someone he'd been friends with since childhood. Swinging his eyes to her other side, he clenched his jaw. J.C. Rousseau. After Alex, the Rousseau brothers were the most notorious flirts of Blueberry Lane. Damn.

Weston on the back as they passed each
looked out at the crowd before letting
again. He smiled at her, then watched,
...e breathless, as her lips tilted up in return. He
...new how those lips tasted, how they felt moving under
his. He intended to relive the experience again as soon as
possible.

"Hi, everyone, and thanks for coming to my brother,
Fitz's, wedding today. I, uh, I had a speech prepared, but if
it's okay with all of you, I thought I'd wing it instead.

"There are millions of people in the world, though not
everyone finds the perfect someone. Not everyone is lucky
enough to find what my brother has found with Daisy.

"But sometimes . . . just when you least expect it, you
might stumble across someone amazing. Someone who
wasn't even on your radar. Someone whom you hope . . ." He
swallowed, still holding Molly's eyes across the room, thinking of her piece of shit fiancé who'd dumped her instead of
accompanying her tonight. "Someone who *gives* you hope
when you'd just about run out of it. And you know . . . someday, it'll happen for you."

He redirected his glance to his brother and sister-in-law,
raising his glass.

"Look at Fitz and Daisy.
It happened for them.
Happy wedding day."

The crowd applauded as Weston took a sip from his glass,
but he didn't see them or hear them. He watched as Molly
stood and quickly edged around her table to a side door
and slipped out of the ballroom. And damn it, if he wasn't
mistaken, she'd swiped at her eyes before she left.

What had he been thinking to make his speech so personal? He'd meant to encourage her to believe that even if
Dusty wasn't "the one," there was someone great out there

for her. There had to be. There had to be someone as amazing *as* Molly *for* Molly.

Politely accepting congratulations and kind wishes, he followed her as quickly as he could, relieved when the band started playing again and couples filed out onto the dance floor. Flicking a quick glance at Molly's table, he locked eyes with J.C. Rousseau, who looked at him curiously with a dry smirk on his face. Weston almost backtracked to find out if J.C. had said or done anything to upset her, but in his heart, Weston knew it was his words that had struck a chord with Molly . . . because he'd wanted them to.

He peeked into the front parlor, not surprised to see the silhouette of a petite woman in front of the windows in the moonlight, looking out over the snow-covered grounds of Haverford Park. Pausing in the doorway for a moment, he wondered what to say to her.

"Molly . . ." he started, pulling the parlor door shut behind him.

"I didn't see it coming," she said softly with her back to him.

"What do you mean?"

She turned away from the windows to face him, her face glistening with tears. "Dusty. I should have seen it coming."

"Molly, I'm sorry if I said anything that made you sad. I was only trying to remind you not to lose hope."

"It was a beautiful toast," she said, her voice breaking a little.

He crossed the room and reached for her hand, tugging it away from her chest where it was pressed. "Come sit with me. Tell me a little bit about you and Dusty."

"You don't want to hear this," she argued.

"I do," he said simply, surprised to realize it was true.

She let him lead her to a small loveseat where they sat down side by side. He put his arm around her, and Molly dropped her head to his shoulder with a deep sigh.

"When did you meet him?" he asked.

"Second grade."

"*What?*"

"Mm-hm. We were both seven. He was the new kid in town. He pulled on my braids and gave me a toothless smile."

"That's all it took, huh? I could have Stratton knock out a couple of my teeth for you if that's your thing . . ."

"Don't you dare," she said, laughing softly. But he felt the lightness of the moment recede quickly as she took a deep breath. "We started dating in high school. Went to OSU together. Went to OSU grad school together. We both wanted to be teachers."

"Is that what you do?" he said. "Teach?"

She nodded against his shoulder. "Yeah. I got my teaching certificate and applied to Teach for America right away. My parents and siblings didn't like it much. They all live close together, have Sunday dinner every week. They're in and out of each other's homes . . . and lives. It caused a rift when I first left, but over the months, we've mended it. I'd always talked about teaching at an inner-city school, but I don't think they really thought I'd go."

"Your family doesn't approve of you working in Philadelphia?" he asked, thinking that he and Molly had a lot more in common than he'd originally guessed. She'd just had the strength to stand up for what she wanted, while he still wrestled with what to do.

"I work in *North* Philly," she said meaningfully. "Near Strawberry Mansion."

"Oh. Oh, wow." Weston leaned back a little so he could look into her eyes. He knew his face probably looked surprised and concerned, but he couldn't help the sudden protectiveness that surged for her. "That's a bad neighborhood, Molly. That's a *dangerous* neighborhood."

"It's not the best," she agreed.

It was none of his business, but he hated the thought of Molly heading to North Philadelphia every day where school shootings were more and more common, and gang violence was prevalent. He'd done extensive research on the North Philly neighborhood of Strawberry Mansion for an ancillary class on forensics and knew that the crime rates there were well above the national average.

"I don't like it."

"Neither did Dusty," said Molly in a tired voice. "He was appalled the one time he came to visit, in fact. He couldn't understand why I'd choose to be here instead of at home, teaching at Hopeview High."

Weston hated to feel any camaraderie with Dusty, so he desperately needed to understand her reason for choosing such a high-risk place to work.

"I'm not sure I do, either."

"I want to make a difference."

Molly had no idea, of course, of the searing impact of her words on Weston. Like her, he wanted to make a difference in the world, specifically by working in the juvenile department of the DA's office, supporting the principle of balance and restorative justice for underage and first-time offenders.

I want to make a difference.

He rolled the words around in his head, savoring them, in awe of them. Six words that summed up Weston's dreams. How he envied and admired Molly for *living* them.

". . . kids who live in Strawberry Mansion deserve just as much of a chance as the kids growing up in Hopeview, Ohio. They are angry and difficult, and I will never get through to some of them. But, there are some who are . . . exceptional. They turn their faces up to me and listen in spite of themselves. They pretend to be bored, but then turn in amazing homework assignments. Out of nowhere they'll share a thought or a feeling about a book I'm teaching, and I swear to God, it's a rush like you wouldn't believe."

Weston was utterly floored by the passion in her voice. He couldn't remember the last time he heard someone discuss their work with such enthusiasm, such satisfaction and excitement. He looked into her eyes, shining with promise and thought, *I want what you have.*

"What?" she asked, furrowing her brow. "You think I'm a zealot?"

"I think you're amazing," he whispered.

"Oh." She smiled in surprise or relief, maybe, but her smile faded quickly. "Dusty didn't." Then she added softly, "You know . . . it's not all his fault."

"Aw, please. *Please* don't do that, Molly. He cheated on you. He's a shitbag excuse for a—"

"I agree," she said. "He's a terrible person for cheating on me. But, I think he had this vision of us teaching side by side at Hopeview High, and I had this vision of teaching in an inner-city school somewhere. If I'm being honest, I need to admit it's possible that while his plan included me, mine may not have included him."

Weston's fingers caressed the ball of her shoulder gently. "Then he should've broken up with you."

"Agreed." She nodded again, but he didn't hear her breathing hitch like tears had started. In fact, she took a smooth, deep breath and sighed. "Thanks for listening. It helped to talk about it."

"Anytime."

"I keep pulling you away from your brother's wedding."

"I follow you willingly every time," he murmured, pressing his lips to her head. "Besides, you're making it less horrible for me, remember?"

"It's your turn to tell me . . . the girl who was supposed to come with you tonight. What happened?"

Her voice was sweet and kind, and he sensed her interest in him was as true and compassionate as his has been a few moments before. But the thing was, he had no interest in talking about Connie. In fact, what had happened with Connie this morning felt like a million years ago. Molly McKenna had happened since, and right now, right here, he only wanted to concentrate on her.

"Another time," he said, kissing her head again. "Hey, Molly McKenna, who is crazy enough and amazing enough to go teach kids in North Philly every day to make a difference . . . are you brave enough to dance with an English brother?"

Chapter 8

As luck would have it, the band was playing another one of her favorite songs from *Singin' in the Rain* called "You Were Meant for Me" as they made their way back into the ballroom hand in hand.

Weston led her onto the dance floor, pulling her expertly into his arms, and she considered how odd it was to have arrived at the church so angry and forlorn, only to find herself swaying gently on the dance floor with Daisy's brother-in-law several hours later. His words during the toast, *Someone who gives you hope, when you'd just about run out of it. And you know . . . someday, it'll happen for you,* had been meant for her, but it was *Weston*—with his hot kisses and kindness and conversation—that was making her believe they were true.

Dusty isn't the end of the line, she told herself. Molly didn't have a clue who she'd end up with, but some small part of her was relieved that Dusty wasn't the one. In a strange turn of events, gratitude was starting to rear its lovely head and remind her that everything happens for a reason. She and Dusty weren't meant to be, and when Molly separated out the humiliation from the actual breakup, she realized some part of her was grateful to be free.

"Penny for your thoughts," said Weston.

No. He'd been kind enough to listen to her talk about Dusty twice now. She wasn't going to let Dusty steal any more time from her and Weston tonight.

"I love this song," she said, grinning at him.

"It's from my mom's favorite movie," confided Weston.

"Mine too!"

"Your favorite or your mom's favorite?"

"My mom's," exclaimed Molly.

"*You look lovely in the moonlight*, Molly," said Weston, trying not to laugh.

She laughed *for* him. The line he'd recited came right before the song they were dancing to in the movie. "How many times have you seen it?"

"Five thousand and fifty-eight," he answered, deadpan. "You?"

"At least that many. Any time it was on TBS or PBS, every Christmas day, every time it rained . . . the list goes on and on."

"I feel your pain."

"It's not that bad . . . *the angels must have sent you and they meant you just for me* . . ."

Realizing that she'd just broken into an impromptu sing-along, she felt her cheeks flush hot, and drew her bottom lip between her teeth sheepishly.

His eyes, which had watched her with surprise as she sang the words, immediately dropped to her lips and lingered there. When his eyes cut back to her, his were stormy, and his voice was low and gravelly when he said, "If dinner wasn't about to start, I'd drag you up the back staircase again."

Molly sucked in a breath, her eyes widening as she stared back at him, wishing they had hours until dinner. The music ended, and Weston stopped dancing, but he held onto her, standing on the edge of the dance floor. He stared at her face as though he were memorizing it, and Molly, captivated by the intensity in his gaze, was helpless to do anything but stare back. He was so beautiful with his wild eyes and a lock of his blond hair falling over his forehead. She reached up and raked her fingers slowly through it, feeling his eyes on her, hot and hungry, until her fingers stilled on the back of his neck.

"Stables after dinner?" he asked softly, making no move to let her go.

Molly licked her lips and pursed them, nodding, stunned by the equal amounts of tenderness and lust she felt for him.

His hands loosened on her lower back, and she suddenly released the breath she'd been holding. What in the world was happening to her?

Taking her hand, he walked her over to her table, pulling out her chair.

"Wes!" said Brooks Winslow, oldest brother of Alex's girl-friend, Jessica, and Weston's sometimes riding companion. "Congratulations on your new sister-in-law. Daisy's a vision."

"Thanks, Brooks."

"Fitz is one lucky bastard," added Preston.

The rest of the table offered their own versions of con-gratulations and good cheer as Molly settled in her seat.

"You've returned our Molly," said J.C., lifting his glass and winking at her. "*Un seul être vous manque et tout est dépeuplé.*"

Molly laughed nervously, wishing she knew what J.C. had said and feeling a little embarrassed by so much attention.

When Weston didn't say anything, she twisted her neck to glance up at him standing behind her chair and was sur-prised to find his expression way beyond icy—it was posi-tively glacial as he looked back at J.C., and Molly sensed it relayed a message that J.C., with his smug grin, read loud and clear.

Finally, Weston cut his eyes to Molly. She watched his face soften as he leaned down and kissed her cheek.

"See you later?"

She smiled and nodded, and with one more warning glance at J.C., Weston turned and headed to his own table.

Weston's French was rusty, but roughly translated, J.C. had said, "With the loss of one person, the whole world can feel empty," as he winked at Molly. It had been on the tip of Weston's tongue to tell J.C. to fuck off and find another girl, but at the last minute, Weston realized he had no claim to Molly. He liked her very much. He hated the fact that he had to leave her with a smooth-talking Frenchman while he fulfilled his filial duties at a table across the room from her. And he'd likely be on edge until her hand was safely laced with his again. But laying claim to her? Weston had no right, and for whatever indecipherable reason, it frustrated him.

Damn J.C. Rousseau to hell and back! Why had Daisy sat Molly beside him anyway? Wasn't there any room at his grandmother's table, for God's sake?

Weston stalked angrily to the table where Barrett and Emily, Fitz and Daisy, Alex and Jessica, Stratton and Valeria, and his cousin, Kate, waited for him. Taking a seat between Kate and Alex, he was further frustrated to discover that his back was to Molly's table and huffed softly as he sat down.

"Well, hello, sunshine," said Kate, nudging him with her elbow.

"Hey, Kate," Weston mumbled, picking up his pre-set champagne flute and downing it.

"Someone's having a great time, huh?"

Weston sighed deeply, looking up to his brothers and their significant others all staring at him. When he saw the worry in Daisy's eyes from across the table, he forced himself to smile warmly at her before turning to Kate.

"Yep, I am, cuz. Thanks for noticing. I'm having a great time."

"I don't miss anything. I'm a litigator."

"Bottom feeder," he teased.

"Just wait 'til you pass the bar, little one. Words like that will be akin to cannibalism." Kate grinned at Weston, grabbed a bottle of white wine from the middle of the table, and poured him a full glass. "That should help."

Weston shrugged, feeling fairly certain that it would take more than a glass of wine to "help." Now, a glass of wine thrown in J.C.'s face? *That* might help.

"Daisy's awfully sweet," Kate whispered into his ear as conversations resumed around the table. "But she doesn't know you like I do. Spill it. What's going on?"

"You know the Rousseaus at all, Kate?"

He was surprised to see her wince lightly before answering. "A little."

"What do you want to know about the Rousseaus?" asked Alex from Weston's other side, flicking a concerned glance at Kate before leveling his eyes on Weston.

"Butt in much?" asked Weston belligerently.

Alex shook his head and Weston noted that his lip was puffy with a touch of dried blood near the spot where it had split.

"You're such a brat tonight," said Alex.

"Yeah? Well, you're a pain in the ass every night."

"Who is? Alex?" asked Barrett, leaning over Kate to join the conversation.

"Wes wants to know what we think of the Rousseaus."

From across the table, Stratton's head snapped up from canoodling with Valeria. "We think they're assholes."

Alex chuckled and lifted his glass to toast Stratton.

"Jax and Mad aren't all bad," said Kate, lifting her chin. "I've always liked them."

"I'm not talking about Jax and Mad," clarified Weston. "Or Ten. Everyone *knows* he's a dick."

Stratton's eyes narrowed as he nodded emphatically, but when Valeria leaned up and kissed his cheek, his whole expression changed on a dime and he beamed down at her with wonder and tenderness.

"Étienne's the worst of the bunch," agreed Alex, throwing back a hefty sip of scotch and winking at Kate.

Weston wasn't sure what was going on between Alex and Kate, but now wasn't the time to find out. J.C. Rousseau was Barrett's age, which meant that Barrett probably knew him best. He leaned over Kate a little. "Barrett, what's J.C. like?"

"Solid businessman. Good with figures. Brokers international deals between—"

"Sweetheart," said Barrett's fiancée, Emily, gently. "That's not what Wes is asking."

"What's he asking?"

Emily's eyes widened and she licked her lips.

"Oh," said Barrett, his whole body shifting closer to Emily. "Oh."

"Barrett?" said Weston. "I'm over here."

Barrett turned back to Weston, but his eyes were darker and Weston noticed his hand snake out and grab Emily's, pulling it possessively into his lap.

"What's he like with women? Charming. Smooth. He dated Hope for a while before Alex did. But, I don't hear bad things about him. He's certainly no Étienne . . ."

Kate cleared her throat, and stood up, excusing herself to go to the bathroom, which meant that Weston could lean over her seat to talk to Barrett.

". . . but he's no choirboy either," finished Barrett.

"Speaking of the Rousseaus," said Jessica, "did you hear that Étienne Rousseau was in an accident a few nights ago?"

Fitz, who sat beside her, nodded. "I did. I heard it was pretty bad, but I don't know any details."

Jessica grimaced, running her finger around the rim of her wineglass. "I don't want to spread gossip, but Brooks told me the police found his car wrapped around a tree and Ten was completely unconscious."

"Jesus," exclaimed Stratton, shaking his head and looking down at the table.

"That's terrible," offered Emily.

Jessica nodded, and they all settled into a maudlin silence, contemplating Étienne Rousseau, who wasn't a good person, but didn't deserve life-threatening injuries, either.

"Wow. Moody bunch. What'd I miss?" asked Kate, returning to the table.

"Nothing," said Alex quickly.

"Absolutely nothing," added Stratton on top of Alex.

"Hey, Wes," asked Daisy, looking eager to change the subject. "What do you think of Molly?"

"Mol-ly!" said Kate in that teasing, singsong voice that girls always used when talking about potential love interests for their brothers or male cousins.

"Ohhhh," said Alex. "Molly? Is that her name? Is that who I have to thank for this?" He pointed to his lip, giving Weston a sour look.

"I'll make it better, baby," said Jessica, palming Alex's face and kissing him gently.

Weston rolled his eyes. "Can you two get a room? I'm sure Alex's is free. And hey! In about ten minutes, I'll come knocking on the door to interrupt you two for more pictures. How about it?"

"We'd be done by then," said Alex in a low, throaty voice, before kissing his fiancée again.

Because Alex and Jess were dissolving into a full-blown make-out session, Weston looked up at his new sister-in-law. "She's great, Daisy."

"I know."

"How did you two meet?"

"We're in a drama club together in Bryn Mawr, near where she lives. Neither of us was cast this season so we split the job of stage manager. I've spent a lot of time with her in the dark," said Daisy, chuckling, her blue eyes sparkling with mischief. "She's better than great. She's terrific, Wes."

Weston quickly processed the thought that he wouldn't mind spending a lot of time in the dark with her too, then shifted uncomfortably in his chair as his body heated up at the thought. When he finally looked back up at Daisy, she was staring at him meaningfully and he easily read the message in her eyes: *Molly deserves better than the jerk who just dumped her*. He nodded at her. He couldn't agree more.

"Well, dating Molly, whoever she is, has got to be better than dating an Atwell sister," said Stratton bluntly, while Barrett and Alex muttered, "Amen, brother," in unison.

"Sorry things didn't work out with Connie," said Fitz, realizing that someone should offer condolences.

Weston shrugged, picking up his fork as the servers finished delivering the salad course. "It wasn't meant to be."

"Thank God," murmured Alex, sighing with relief.

"You have to admit, Christmases would have been awkward," noted Barrett, as they all eschewed conversation for dinner.

They weren't meant to be, him and Connie, and it startled him how much the realization didn't sting—how right it felt in his heart to be finished with her.

Knowing his possessive nature, Connie had still made it her goal in life—every time they went out together—to arouse his jealousy. If they were at a dance club, she'd say yes, then rub up against the random man who asked her to dance. If she accompanied Weston to a horse show, she'd disappear for thirty minutes only to reappear plucking a piece of straw from her hair with a cat-that-got-the-cream smirk. When her phone buzzed with a text, she'd giggle coyly, sucking her bottom lip into her mouth as she quickly typed a response, then sighing as she waited for an answer. She was always playing these little games with him— making him think one thing, then making him apologize when it turned out to be untrue. Connie liked his jealousy. She goaded it. She encouraged it. Hell, half the time she probably engineered it. Why? Why did she want him to be jealous? Did she like the arguments? Did she like fighting with him?

And then it occurred to him . . . this morning, he'd referenced their fights, saying that they'd let "stupid shit" come between them, but Connie hadn't addressed those concerns. All Connie had asked about, several times, were his feelings for her: what did he feel for her and did he love her. Was that it, then? Was she just goading him into jealousy to try and figure out his feelings for her?

In his heart, Weston suddenly knew—with absolute certainty—that it was true. He'd never loved Connie, but she had loved him, and making him jealous was her way of trying to nail down his feelings. But the truth was that Weston had never crossed over from jealousy to love. He'd see her or imagine her with someone else, and it would make him angry. They'd throw insults at each other and have a big fight. One of them would leave. A few weeks or months later, they'd run into each other and fall into bed again.

But love? No. Love had never been a part of the equation at all because Weston's jealousy wasn't about loving Connie. It was about proving something that had nothing to do with her. It was Weston, the youngest English brother, trying to prove he was just as good as any other man. It was Weston longing to be first when he'd always be fifth.

With startling clarity he realized that until he made a clean break from his brothers and his family in some real way, he'd always be jealous and longing. Jealous of something he longed for, but by virtue of birth order could never, ever have. If he wanted a fallow field, he was going to need to find it himself. He was going to have to make it happen on his own.

Turning in his seat, he looked across the room, searching for Molly's red head in the candlelit room. Her back was to him, but his heart surged when he found her. He thought of her determination and bravery. Somehow she'd summoned the courage to follow her dream: to leave her parents farm, risk her engagement and disappoint her family. All because she wanted to make a difference, because she wanted something no one else in her life respected or understood. She came to Philadelphia alone and set forth every day from lovely Bryn Mawr to the treacherous world of Strawberry Mansion, hoping that today was the day one of her students' faces would light up with understanding, and she'd redirect the course of one of their lives.

And suddenly Weston felt like one of her students, learning from her example, and desperate to apply her wisdom to his own life.

The bar was in two weeks.

He shifted back toward his family and quietly circled the table with his eyes: Barrett, so stern and strong; Stratton, with his clumsy words and brilliant mind; Fitz, who was their conscience and backbone; and Alex, whose charm and twinkling eyes could sell sawdust to a lumber mill.

The problem wasn't Weston's future. At some point tonight, the die had been cast, the scale had been tipped, the decision had been made. Deep inside of Weston, he knew he wouldn't be going to work for English & Sons in two weeks after passing the bar. He'd be applying for a position at the Philadelphia district attorney's office. And with his education and family name, he had no doubt there would be a position for him. He enjoyed the thrill of this momentous decision for just a moment before an immense heaviness descended.

No, the problem wasn't Weston's dream for his future. The problem was he was going to have to break his brother's hearts to make it come true.

Chapter 9

Molly shook her head at J.C. with a grin, wondering how often his lines worked and on what type of woman they were effective. Not that she was totally immune. Was he tempting? Yes. With his dark hair and hooded eyes, he looked the way she envisioned one of her favorite romance heroes, Gideon Cross. Powerful, sexy, and magnetic, J.C. Rousseau was probably every woman's dream of the perfect man.

Except that Molly's head was captivated by a different look entirely, and she couldn't shake it. Tousled blond hair, intense blue eyes, and an altogether younger face were dominating her brain, despite J.C.'s efforts to charm her. More than anything, Molly wanted to reconnect with Weston again. As soon as possible.

Which is why, when she saw him take to the dance floor with a gorgeous blonde bridesmaid between the salad and main courses, her heart fell.

His dance partner was lovely.

Blonde and blue-eyed, she looked far more sophisticated than farm-raised Molly, her hair twisted up in a tasteful chignon and creamy pearls nestled against her tan skin.

Molly drew a shaky breath, reviewing that Weston had four brothers and no sisters, and so she assumed the beauty was one of Daisy's friends. Weston smiled into her eyes with ease, throwing his head back at one point to laugh at something she said. Molly's fist clenched in her lap and she turned sharply around to face the table.

"Mmm," murmured J.C., glancing at Weston before inclining his head to Molly. "Weston is dancing with Kate, I see."

She looked at her dinner partner. "Kate?"

"Mm-hm. And she has changed quite a bit, hasn't she? Much improved."

"I don't know Kate," said Molly, practically spitting out her name and hating the way her stomach clenched into a knot.

Why would Weston want to spend any more of his brother's wedding with dumped, sad-sack Molly when he could spend time with "much improved" Kate? Molly snuck another glance at the stunning blonde, only to see Weston lean down to whisper something in Kate's ear. She gave him a look, shaking her head like he was being a bad boy, then giggled, dropping her forehead on his shoulder.

Molly's cheeks flared, and she turned back around.

Stop looking. Stop torturing yourself.

"Kate's been a favorite of the English family forever," said J.C. smoothly, his eyes mischievous as he picked up his wine glass to take a sip. "Their families are . . . entrenched. Entwined."

Molly's eyes widened, searching J.C.'s face, but she could tell that he was telling the truth. Whoever Kate was to Weston, they'd known one another for a long time and there appeared to be a deep affection and ease between them.

"Do Weston and Kate . . . have history?"

"Yes," said J.C. gravely, his face telegraphing his sympathy for her. "Quite a lot, I'm afraid. A very close and intimate history that goes all the way to their births."

"So, he's loved her forever?" asked Molly in a dazed voice, feeling a burn behind her eyes.

"Forever? Oh, yes. *Absolument.*"

Unlike Molly, who had no prospects waiting for her after Dusty's betrayal, Weston had had Kate in the wings. His girlfriend dumps him this morning, he dallies with Molly for an hour or two, then makes his move on picture-perfect Kate.

"How efficient," said Molly under her breath, reaching for her glass and gulping down the contents.

Placing her empty glass back on the table, Molly took a deep breath, feeling like all sorts of an idiot and hating that she felt dumped for the second time in two days, even though she had no right to feel that way. Weston didn't owe her anything; he didn't belong to her. They'd shared a few kisses, and honestly, he'd been kind to her. She should be grateful for that much.

She had no right to expect anything else from him.

And yet, despite the terrible timing of their meeting tonight, Molly wanted more. After knowing the hot sweetness of his smile and the gentleness of his eyes as he listened to her, the way he held her in his arms and kissed her like the world was ending . . . it made it unexpectedly difficult for her to accept that their short, sweet liaison was over.

Looking back over at the dance floor, she watched Weston stare at Kate with deep tenderness after she whispered something in his ear. Stopping middance, he pulled her flush against him, embracing her tightly. When his eyes darted in the direction of Molly's table, they bypassed Molly, lingering on J.C. Rousseau with marked disdain, before turning back to Kate. Weston reached up and palmed her cheek, smiling at her with deep emotion, before taking her hand and walking her back to their table.

Molly's breath caught from the blow of their exchange— she'd read love, tenderness, compassion, and protectiveness in Weston's gaze. The way he'd held her, the way they touched each other so familiarly . . . it was clear: Kate was *very* important to Weston.

Angry, bitter Molly from earlier in the night suddenly raised her brittle head. She had no right to the jealousy she felt, but she couldn't help it. Her head said she had no claim on Weston, but her heart virulently disagreed. First Dusty, now Weston. There was only one solution to waylay tears: move on. Quickly.

Her heart thumping almost uncomfortably, she turned to J.C., affecting her best smile and licking her lips before pulling the bottom one between her teeth. "Do you care to dance?"

He looked surprised only for an instant before smiling at her, his white teeth perfect behind sexy, pillowed lips. "With you, *mignon*? *Oui*. Yes."

"Great."

Molly stood upright without giving him a moment to help her with her chair, and she didn't look at him as she took his hand.

J.C. led her to the dance floor, smoothly weaving around tables as they made their way, and Molly followed closely behind him, keeping her eyes fastened on the shoulder of his navy blue suit. Once on the dance floor, he pulled her into his arms possessively, holding her very close with his arms around her waist rather than in a traditional dancing pose. Something in Molly protested this liberty as she placed her hands on his shoulders. But when her mind flashed back to Weston dancing with Kate, she pressed herself forward against the hardness of J.C.'s chest, and looped her arms around the back of his neck.

Resting her cheek on his shoulder, she felt his hot breath against her neck, moving against her hair as they barely moved to the Beatles' "Here, There and Every-where." His hands laced together on her lower back and

Molly clenched her jaw in defiance of his touch, feeling utterly miserable.

"Molly," he whispered. "You're a wonderful dancer. We should go out together sometime."

"Sure," she agreed quietly, wishing her eyes weren't burning and her heart wasn't longing for someone else's arms.

"Next weekend?"

"Why not?" she murmured, hating that a sexy, intimate dance with a Gideon Cross lookalike wasn't enough to make her forget the rogue lock of Weston's blond hair running through her fingers.

J.C.'s chest heaved, and his cheek brushed hers as he pulled back to look into her eyes. His dark eyes flicked a glance at her lips in question before tilting his head to the side and—

"I'm cutting in."

Molly sputtered in surprise, shocked to hear Weston's voice laced with fury so close to her ear.

J.C.'s body tensed, pulling back from Molly's just a little, like he'd been caught doing something wrong. But his face remained impassive as he flicked his hand at Weston like an annoying bug. "Go away, *petit* Weston."

"I have already punched Alex twice tonight, and he's my brother. I promise you, I will rearrange your face if you don't let go of her right now."

J.C. turned his gaze to Molly. "*Mignon?*"

Molly ignored J.C. and stared back at Weston, confusion dominating her other feelings of hope, anger, and relief. She cocked her head to the side. "Why don't you dance with Kate some more? You two seemed pretty cozy."

"Kate?" Weston demanded, his face shocked and incredulous.

"Yes, Kate. *Entwined, improved Kate* who you've known *intimately* for years, and *loved forever*."

Weston looked at J.C., holding his eyes with fury. "You told her that?"

"It's not the truth?"

Molly didn't know what was going on, but she let her hands fall from around J.C.'s neck as she watched his face segue from mischievous to sheepish. She darted her eyes to Weston, who looked disgusted with J.C. and more furious by the minute. He finally cut his humorless, searing eyes to Molly.

"Kate's my cousin, Molly. Our fathers are brothers. Kate's the closest thing I have to a sister and she just shared something with me"—his eyes darted, with hatred, to J.C.—"from her past. Me embracing Kate? That was just me comforting my cousin."

"Oh . . ." Molly sighed, closing her eyes and shaking her head in embarrassment. *Oh, God, I wish I could turn back time.* "I thought—"

"I know exactly what you thought," said Weston, taking her hand and pulling her away from J.C., who released her with a vaguely amused, mildly guilty shrug.

He finally smirked, putting his hands in his pockets. "*Tout est juste dans l'amour et la guerre.*"

"This wasn't love but it could be war," said Weston, his tone thick with disgust. He tucked Molly against his side, his arm tight around her shoulders. "*Another* Rousseau brother being a total asshole."

"Ah, Weston. You English brothers take yourselves so seriously. We French have far more fun." J.C. winked at Molly before turning away from them and sauntering back to the table.

"Yeah. That was super fun," said Weston, still stewing as he eyed J.C.'s retreat.

"It was my fault," Molly whispered.

"It was *his* fault," he murmured, staring into her eyes. "Dance with me?"

She nodded and Weston pulled her into his arms as a new slow song, Billy Joel's "She's Always a Woman," started playing. Just as J.C. had a moment before, Weston laced his hands on Molly's lower back, but this time her body, finally paired with the man she wanted, relaxed in gratitude, and she rested her cheek on his shoulder, breathing deeply and closing her eyes.

His scent was a mix of messy sheets, something lightly spicy, and a faint hint of hay, which made Molly's heart sigh with pleasure. Her hands slid up his chest to his shoulders, meeting at the back of his neck, which she grazed with her fingers, the heat of his skin burning her tender tips.

"Molly," he whispered, slowly and gently against her ear. "How could you think I'd—"

"I barely know you," she answered, and she imagined her words deflected off the throbbing pulse in his throat.

"That's not true."

"I only met you a few hours ago," she insisted, even though she agreed with him. In a relatively short time, they'd somehow bonded far more than she would have thought possible.

But the timing was dreadful, as evidenced by her gullibility. Molly's heart wasn't ready for this much action. She'd barely processed Dusty's betrayal and rejection. It wasn't prudent to open her heart to someone else. She didn't want to feel jealous of Weston, possessive of Weston, tender toward Weston. She needed perspective. She needed to protect herself—give her heart a chance to heal before opening it up to the possibility of more pain.

Sensible Molly, who had been sidelined for a good portion of the evening, was suddenly awake and full of energy, while Wild Molly was starting to feel a little beat up. Sensible Molly patted Wild Molly on the head, rubbing her back with maternal compassion and urged her to go take a rest.

"It doesn't matter how long ago we met," said Weston. "I like you. I think you like me. I want to—"

"I'm sorry, Weston," she murmured, the slow swaying so comfortable and easy, she hated the words that came out of her mouth next. "The timing is all wrong here."

"What do you mean?"

She swallowed the lump in her throat, trying to savor the last few bars of the song, the feeling of his arms around her, the touch of his breath so close to her throat.

You're just scared. Don't do it, said Wild Molly in a thin, barely there voice.

"I mean," she said, opening her eyes and gathering her Sensible Molly strength, "that it's time for me to go."

His face instantly clouded over in protest. "But I told you. Kate's just my cousin. Please don't go. You were going to stay and we were going to—"

"I'm sorry," she said again, lowering her hands from his neck to hang loosely at her sides. "It's just too much."

He bit down on his bottom lip, staring at her with dismay. "What can I say?"

"Good-bye."

"This is ridiculous."

I think so, too, said Wild Molly, almost too softly to hear.

"I think it's for the best," she said, reaching behind her back to loosen his hands.

He let go of her, clenching his jaw, his eyes smoldering with anger and frustration. "Fine. Go."

She stepped away from him, then stopped, looking into his beautiful eyes, sweeping her gaze over the hard lines of his face. Wincing at the hurt and rejection she saw there, she was overwhelmed with regret and confusion and too many other uncomfortable feelings to process on the dance floor of his brother's wedding.

"Thanks for making tonight not so horrible," she said softly, in a broken voice.

Then she turned away quickly, leaving him standing alone in the middle of the dance floor.

Did it make sense? No. Did anything? No. Had he ever experienced frustration quite on this particular plane before? No.

All he knew was that watching Molly walk away from him hurt far worse than Connie breaking up with him this morning. It reminded him of the way Alex used to sucker punch him when he was a kid. His belly, so soft and relaxed, wouldn't have time to brace for the assault of Alex's balled fist. It hurt ten times as much, knocking the wind from his chest and making his eyes water.

And that's exactly what happened now. His chest felt tight and his eyes watered, and he couldn't account for it, except to say that the few hours he'd spent with Molly weren't nearly enough, and he felt incredibly shortchanged. It was only nine-thirty and there were still hours left in Fitz's wedding. Hours he'd wanted to spend with her.

He didn't go back to his table, despite the fact that dinner was being served. He slipped out of the room and beelined for his father's study, where he uncapped a bottle of good scotch and poured himself a shot. After tossing it back he poured another, sitting down heavily in his father's leather easy chair as the liquor scorched a soothing path to his stomach.

What was it about Molly McKenna that was so suddenly and completely addictive to Weston?

Her beauty? Sure. She was fresh-faced, sexy, and stunning.

The heat between them? Absolutely. Weston had been with quite a few women, but he could honestly say he'd never generated as much heat with any of them as he had over the last few hours with Molly.

That she'd been dumped by such an asshole riled his protective nature. But it was more than her looks or their chemistry or the fact that she was having a bad day. Molly was a remarkable person—growing up on a little farm in Ohio, she pushed herself through grad school, only to accept a job at an underprivileged school in North Philly all so she could make a difference. Molly was someone really, really worth knowing. And it pissed him off that their time had been cut short.

He briefly thought about striding into the ballroom and punching J.C. Rousseau in the face for misleading Molly and upsetting her so much. Especially after learning from Alex that Étienne Rousseau had not only taken Kate's virginity but rejected her afterwards, Weston was eager to hurt one of the Rousseaus and J.C. had given him cause. But he thought of Daisy's sweet face, and regardless of the satisfaction he'd derive in the moment, it wasn't worth casting a pall over her beautiful wedding by getting into another fight. Loyalty to Fitz and Daisy trumped his longing for revenge, and he decided against it.

That decided, he definitely didn't want to go back to the wedding yet. Molly was gone, which made Weston feel more alone than he'd felt all day, and all of the horribleness of being at a wedding was washing over him once again. Except this time, he wasn't even in the mood for a hook-up. There was only one woman he wanted to touch, talk to, and spend time with, and she had left. He considered running after her—she was probably still waiting for the valet to bring her car around—but that smacked of desperation and besides, if she wanted to leave, he needed to let her go. When Fitz and Daisy got back from their honeymoon, he could ask Daisy for Molly's phone number. By then, her breakup from

Dusty would be two weeks in the past, and perhaps she'd be willing to give Weston a chance. He hoped so.

Somewhat mollified, though still unhappy, he decided to head to his room for a few minutes. If he could relieve some of the tension in his body—not that he'd need the cache of magazines under his bed, but they were there just in case—maybe he could get through the last few hours of the wedding without killing someone.

Filling his glass again, he left his father's study and made his way around the ballroom to the grand staircase. From the front vestibule of Haverford Park, which was completely empty except for a doorman, he could hear the soft cacophony of forks and knives in the ballroom, indicating that dinner was in full swing. He trudged up the stairs, feeling grumpy and frustrated, sipping the scotch and wishing that Molly McKenna had stayed.

Arriving at the third floor landing, Weston furrowed his brow to find the door to his room ajar. Perhaps Molly had left it open when he left her for pictures several hours ago? He stepped through the door and blinked with surprise to find Molly sitting on his bed.

Chapter 10

"Molly?"

Her face whipped up in surprise, and her dark eyes widened as two splotches of red suddenly colored her cheeks. "Weston! What are you doing here?"

His lips twitched. "It's my room."

"Of course," she said, her voice a little breathless, her palms reaching up to cover her cheeks.

"I thought you were leaving," he said, stepping into the room and closing the door behind him. His heart thudded with relief, but he was glad the words sounded casual in his ears.

"I was. I am," she said, but she didn't stand up. She sat perched on the edge of his bed, staring at him as he crossed the room toward her. Holding the little purse on her lap, she said, "I left this in your bathroom. It has my valet ticket."

"Oh."

"So I came up here to get it." She shrugged, wetting her lips. Her eyes were weak and wavering, and he swallowed down the hope that he read surrender there too. "But . . ."

He squatted down before her so she wouldn't have to strain her neck to look up at him. "But what?"

"I don't want to go," she said simply, whispering the words with a fraught, resigned tone, like she was sharing an unpleasant secret. "I just . . . downstairs? I felt so over-whelmed, so . . . jealous. I've never felt like that before, and it makes no sense because I have no claim to you. But I—I hated it . . ."

"Seeing me dancing with Kate?" he asked, holding his breath, his stomach fluttering with urgency.

She nodded. "Yes."

Weston's body relaxed and he spoke on a sigh. "I felt the same way when you were dancing with J.C. I wanted to punch something. I couldn't stand seeing his hands on you."

Molly's eyes filled with tears and she swallowed, shaking her head. "I don't want to feel like this. It feels dangerous. It feels like it could hurt me, and I've already been hurt . . ."

He reached forward, wrestling one of her hands away from the purse she was clutching, white-knuckled, on her lap. "My mother used to say . . . you can't help the way you feel. You can only help what you do about it."

She nodded, letting him entwine his fingers through hers, but kept her eyes cast down. "Which is why I thought I should leave."

"No." He shook his head, feeling a wave of tenderness overtake him. "You don't have to leave. Molly, look at me. Please, look at me, sweetheart. J.C. was having some fun with us, that's all. It's not dangerous. I'm not going to hurt you. And I'd love it if you'd stay."

Her furrowed brows eased a bit, and she took a deep, rag-ged breath. "You would?"

"It all got horrible again when you left," he teased, giving her a little grin.

Molly looked concerned, reaching out with her free hand to cup his cheek with her palm. "Did you start thinking about her again? The girl from this morning?"

Terribly distracted by the sweetness of her touch, Weston fought the urge to rest his head in her lap. Instead, he forced himself to pull away from her and stand, taking off his jacket and laying it over his desk chair before sitting beside her on the bed. He offered her his scotch and she took it from him, lifting the glass to her lips for a sip, then wrinkling her nose and handing it back to him quickly.

"Christ on a cracker, that's strong!"

Surprised by her outburst, he chuckled softly as he took the glass from her. His smile faded a little as he got lost staring at her, confused by how relieved he was to find her here, how desperately he wanted her to stay.

"Weston?"

"What?"

"The girl from this morning?"

"Who? Connie? No. No, I'm not sad about her. If this evening has taught me anything, it's that Connie and I weren't meant to be." He scoffed lightly. "I mean, I couldn't fall for you this fast if my heart belonged to her."

Molly gasped and Weston realized what he'd just said. He looked away and considered taking it back, but however unbelievable or inconvenient, the words were true, so he let them stand, raising his eyes to her face as she processed them.

Would she leave? Would she leave now? If she'd been overwhelmed before, this latest declaration wasn't going to help. Suddenly, he felt panicked. Maybe he *should* take them back.

"Molly . . ." he started, but his words were cut short by her lips slamming into his.

When Molly had recovered her purse, she'd also checked her phone for the first time since arriving at the reception, and much to her dismay, there were over a dozen unread text messages from Dusty. Molly had furrowed her brow, staring at the red number fourteen on the phone screen with confusion, because that was a lot of texts, even if Dusty *was* on a mission for forgiveness. For one brief second she considered reading them, which made her furious because it would mean he'd managed to manipulate her into a conversation. She huffed in protest, swiping her index finger over his name and deleted the entire thread without giving them a peek.

The way she was ignoring him was likely driving him crazy. Well, good. She didn't owe him her understanding and forgiveness. But even her little show of spirit wasn't enough to balance the lost and pathetic feelings generated by seeing Dusty's name. She put her phone back in her purse and plopped down dejectedly on Weston's bed.

Weston's bed, however, was possibly the only antidote on earth to feeling dumped and depressed. It was impossible not to respond when Weston's bed smelled like him and a little bit like her too, and vivid memories of their make-out session suddenly flooded her brain and made her weak for an immediate reprise.

Seeing him walk through the door a few minutes later, like the strength of her longing had somehow procured him, appealed to her heart on an almost-fictional level of fate. But hearing the words *I couldn't fall for you this fast if my heart belonged to her* had vaulted her instantly from a mopey place of "maybe" to an empowered place of "yes," because—*Oh, my God*—he was *falling* for her, and never, ever had there been sweeter, prettier, more welcome words to Molly McKenna's recently rejected heart.

Her hands followed her lips to his face, cupping his cheeks with urgency, and Weston reacted instantly, twisting on the bed to face her, gently pushing her back with his body. He lay beside her, his upper chest pushing into hers on an angle and leaning over her to kiss her back as fiercely as she was kissing him.

"Scoot back," he panted, his breath hot on her lips, and Molly lifted her feet to the edge of the mattress for leverage, braced up on her elbows, and pulled her body all the way onto the bed.

Weston rolled on top of her, his elbows on either side of her head and his hands on her cheeks. His body was hard and heavy over hers, but she didn't feel crushed beneath him. She sank into the mattress, loving the contours of his aroused body pressed so intimately against hers. His eyes were darkly sensual, threaded with tenderness when she met them.

"Is this okay?" he asked breathlessly. "Make sure it's okay, because I'm planning to spend a little time right here, Molly."

"It's perfect," she said, tipping her neck back to offer her lips to him.

Weston seized them greedily, sucking the top one between his, only to release it and take the bottom one in the same way, teasing her with morsels when she wanted a meal. When he took her top lip between his again, she bit his bottom one lightly, then licked it quickly, loving it when his breath caught and he ceased games, greedily sealing his lips flush over hers and sweeping her mouth with his tongue. Holding back an urge to laugh with arousal and pleasure and happiness, a sound, deep and low in her throat, emerged like a moan and it was so sexy and unfamiliar in her ears, she arched her body into his.

One hand slipped from her face under her back and skated up to her neck to find her dress zipper and draw it down swiftly. As Molly lay back down, his hand landed on her shoulder, gently skimming against her skin and gliding the strap of her dress down her arm. His lips skipped, like a flat rock on a lake, touching down on her chin, her jaw, her throat, the small of her neck to her bare shoulder, which he kissed gently. His soft, firm lips were heaven against her sensitive skin as his free hand pushed at the dress's scoop neck. Molly leaned up, letting gravity pull the straps down to her elbows before laying back. Weston finished her work, laying a warm palm on her chest, and then smoothing down the dress to her waist.

Molly pulled her arms free, plunging her fingers into the blond waves of his thick hair and sighing as his lips landed on her black lace–covered breast, teasing the already-hard nipple into full erection, which strained against the fabric, frustrated for any barrier between her sensitive skin and the smooth, wet warmth of Weston's mouth. She whimpered as his hand replaced his mouth, kneading and teasing as his lips took the other nipple through the film of lace.

"P-Please," she pleaded with him, her breathing sharp and shallow.

"Shhhh," he murmured against her nipple, making it pucker between his slack lips as they hushed her.

She slid her hands out of his hair and covered his fingers with hers, lacing through, to guide them over her breasts. Once flush, she slipped the tips of her fingers into the top of the lace and pulled down, freeing her breasts to the heaven of his mouth. Her hands smoothed down her stomach, falling flat to the sheets.

Plumping one breast with his hand, his lips fell greedily to her nipple, sucking it into his mouth and swirling his tongue around it again and again as her body arched off the bed, her pelvis, lined up perfectly with his, pressing insistently against his erection as her fingers balled into fists with handfuls of crushed sheet.

"Ohhhh. . . ." she whimpered, biting her bottom lip and clenching her eyes shut as he sucked the second nipple into his mouth—the wet, the warmth, the hungry sucking—making silken webs of pleasure radiate out from her breasts. Goosebumps rose on her skin, and she pressed her head back into the bunched comforter.

His lips kissed a path from her heart to her throat, gently licking the throbbing pulse in her neck before capturing her mouth again, his hips thrusting forward lightly to mimic sex. He threaded his hands through her hair, almost roughly, to move her head how he wanted it.

Her tongue tangled with his and she swallowed his groans, marveling that they'd both lived on the earth for years without knowing she was the magnesium to his fire, the perfect clash of ingredients, combining to create white-hot sparks like lightning. What if they'd never found each other? What if they somehow lost each other?

"Molly, Molly, Molly," he breathed against her ear, taking the soft lobe between his teeth again as he had hours before and making her writhe beneath him from the sharp sweetness. "What do you want? What do you want to do?"

"I want . . ." she panted, skimming her hands from the sheets to his back, feeling the strong, smooth lines of his body under his white shirt, and knowing that his flesh would be hard and hot beneath her fingers as she held him against her as he pushed himself into the greedy heat of her body. "Oh, God, I want . . ."

The muscles deep inside of her body clenched with want. She wanted him. She wanted him to pull off the rest of her clothes and take off his, she wanted him to kiss her whole body the way Dusty never had, the way she'd always craved, and she wanted to feel Weston slide himself into her until she was filled, until he had claimed every last inch of her body, until—

Sensible Molly suddenly appeared out of nowhere.

Are you sure about this? she asked.

"Oh, please," she moaned softly. She *wanted* him. She wanted to feel him—all of him. If his lips on her lips and his lips on her breasts created sparks, surely the feel of his body joined with hers would cause fireworks, hot and glorious and—

"Whatever you want, sweetheart."

Weston lingered by her ear, his hands still molded over her breasts as his thumbs flicked the still damp skin, keeping her so aroused, her blood thundered in her ears, and yet she heard the question again in her head:

ARE. YOU. SURE?

"No," she sobbed tearlessly, letting her hands fall from his back to the sheets with bitter regret. Her frustration extreme, her eyes burned and welled with tears, so she clenched them shut.

Did she want him?

Yes. Every cell in her body was screaming for him.

But her heart, her recently bruised heart, begged her mind to take a beat, to think it over, to be sure that having Weston wasn't a decision she'd deeply regret by tomorrow. She wished she was sure. She wished she was the sort of girl who could sleep with Weston—knowing there was a decent chance it would be a one-night-stand—take her pleasure, and walk away with a smile. She wished she was the sort of girl who wouldn't moon about for the next two weeks, two months, two years, dreaming of him, reliving every moment, waiting for the phone to ring as her heart grew brittle. She wished she wasn't the sort of girl who required a promise, a plan, a "next time." But she was.

Sleeping with him would be risky. But without any sort of indication that their flirtation would last beyond tonight? And bearing in mind she'd been dumped by her fiancé yesterday? It was emotional suicide.

"No?" he murmured against her ear, his body stilling.

"No," she whispered meekly.

"No." He sighed. Not an argument, a resigned confirmation.

"I'm sorry," she said miserably, slack beneath him.

He rolled to his side, and Molly reached up to pull the cups of her bra over her breasts, the cool, wet lace making her shiver.

"Are you cold?"

"A little," she said, covering herself as she sat up, afraid to look at him.

He shuffled a little, into a kneeling position. She watched as he plumped the three pillows, then piled them against the headboard. He sat back with his legs out straight in front of him—the crotch of his pants tented aggressively—then opened his arms and said, "Come here."

His face was hard to read. She saw frustration, disappointment, amusement, tenderness. It was the tenderness that made her inch forward to rest her cheek against his chest and let herself be wrapped in his arms.

"Pull up the comforter," said Weston, and Molly leaned forward, grabbing an end and tugging it over their legs before resettling herself against him. Her dress was still bunched around her waist, but she didn't mind lying against him in her bra. She closed her eyes, breathing him in: messy bed, spice (which she now identified as scotch), and the barest whiff of stable. It was a combination of smells she would always love and always remember—no matter what—as long as she lived.

"You kind of surprised me there," he said. "I was sure we were going to say—"

"I surprised myself," she confessed.

She felt the press of his lips against her head. "Can't say I wasn't hoping."

Molly sighed. "It's just . . . me and Dusty. You and . . . Connie? It all happened so recently, you know? And this is really intense . . . this, this thing between us. I don't want to get hurt. I don't want *you* to get hurt."

"I understand," he said gently, lifting his lips from her head and leaning against the pillows. His fingers ran soothingly up and down her back and she kept her eyes closed, listening to the strong beat of his heart under her ear.

"What happened with Connie?"

"Hmm," he murmured, as though composing his thoughts, his fingers maintaining their gentle up and down rhythm. "I've known Con forever. We grew up together. Same country club. Same hunt club. Same dance instructor. Barrett dated her sister, Felicity, and Alex dated her other sister, Hope."

"Ahhh," said Molly, looping her arm over his chest. "Felicity, Hope, and Constance. The virtues."

"Not really," he said sardonically. "We dated off and on for the past year. We'd be together for a while, and then we'd get into a big fight, say awful things, and go our separate ways. A few weeks or months later, we'd run into each other again and give things another try. Same cycle, over and over."

"You never moved forward."

"What do you mean?"

Molly shrugged. "I don't know . . . one of you would need to bend, you know? When you got into that big fight and said awful things, one of you would need to bend. Say you're sorry. Make amends. Move forward."

Weston nodded and his lips touched down on the crown of her head again. "You're right. Neither of us ever bent, and we never moved forward. We were stuck in the same cycle over and over again. I don't know why."

"My guess is because you weren't in love. You could imagine your lives without each other."

She was right. She was 100 percent, exactly, perfectly right.

He and Constance had heat, but they didn't have love.

"You're pretty smart."

"Not really," she said softly. "I only just realized it, but I'm speaking from experience."

"You and Dusty? Endless fights? Walking away? Somehow I don't see it."

She sniffled softly, and he held her tighter as a surge of protectiveness made him almost breathless. What was it about this girl that was so compelling to him? How did she pull at more heartstrings after five hours than Constance had in over a year?

Her voice was soft and measured when she continued. "We didn't fight much. We didn't say ugly things. But I thought them, and I'm sure he did too. And we both walked away. Figuratively and literally. I think my engagement was over the day I took the job in Philly and he watched me go. I just didn't realize it at the time."

"He was a fool to let you go."

She shook her head, the light brushing of her cheek against his chest more affecting than any other woman grabbing his junk.

"No," she said in a quiet, accepting voice. "Somewhere inside of Dusty he knew I wasn't the one. He just *wished* I was. He liked the idea of us. That's why he's . . ."

"Why he's what?"

She started to say something else, then shook her head. "Nothing. I don't want to talk about him, okay?"

"Yeah. Okay."

They were silent for several long minutes after that, and Weston became distinctly aware of her breathing, the way her chest pushed lightly into his as she inhaled, the way her fingers lightly flexed and relaxed against his waist. Her hair smelled sweet, like the Wisteria that grew over the arches at the entrance to his mother's rose garden. He inhaled it, and it reminded him of warm summer days, of blue skies, of clean slates and fresh starts, sweet smiles and gentle touches. Would he still know Molly four months from now when the arbors were in full bloom, their lavender tendrils hanging low and bathing the air in sweetness? Suddenly it seemed unbearable to imagine that he wouldn't know her, that she wouldn't somehow be a part of his life four days from now, four months from now, four years from now, four whatever-else's, anything-else's from right now.

Like other people on the planet, he'd heard of men who said that they met a pretty girl one day, and felt it in their gut with a certainty that couldn't be denied: *This is the girl I'm going to marry*. But he never, ever thought such a fanciful thing would happen to him.

And yet. Here he was. Five hours in, and no way to turn back.

And all he wanted to do, suddenly, was make sure that Molly McKenna would linger in his life beyond tonight. *It's Saturday*, he thought. *Would a date for dinner tomorrow night be too soon?*

"Mol—"

"Wes—"

He chuckled softly. "You go first, sweetheart."

"You got really high marks on your LSAT," she said.

He furrowed his brow, but grinned with pleasure. He wasn't expecting that, but he realized with her cheek against his chest, she was staring straight at his desk.

"I guess. Not perfect, though."

"When we were in the tack room, you said you didn't want to be a corporate lawyer for English & Sons."

"Mm-hm," he conceded, his jaw tightening.

"What *do* you want to do?"

He tensed, just a little, because he'd never shared his dreams aloud. Before tonight, he'd never even admitted that he didn't want to follow his brothers into the family firm. Was he ready to tell someone what he really wanted to do?

Not surprisingly, surrounded by the magic that was Molly McKenna, the words came quickly and cleanly. Regardless of the hurt it would cause, he wouldn't be working at English & Sons.

"I want to work in the Philadelphia district attorney's office. Ideally in the juvenile division."

"Wes," she murmured, sitting up straighter to look at him.

He searched her eyes, wondering what she was thinking, wondering if she thought he was crazy for turning his back on his family's venerable business.

"Tell me more," she said, her eyes flooded with admiration, her lips tilting up just slightly.

He swallowed, his bravery bolstered by her encouragement. "I had this professor in law school . . . my advisor, actually, who served in the DA's office. Professor Callum told us a lot of stories about kids—first-time offenders who made bad choices and screwed up their lives. And I just don't believe that a sixteen-year-old arrested for armed robbery should go to prison for twenty years. I think there's got to be another way, a better way, to rehabilitate that person. But first he's going to need a decent defense, and I . . . well, I . . ."

"You want to make a difference," said Molly, her wide eyes skimming over his face like a caress, like he was the most beautiful thing she'd ever seen.

He nodded, dropping his lips to hers just for a moment before pulling away. "I do."

Her eyes fluttered opened slowly and she smiled at him, her face so utterly lovely, his breath caught. "I think *you're* amazing."

For a moment—just a moment—he let himself bask in the warm glow of her admiration, soaking it up like sunshine and tucking it away into the corner of his heart that would belong to her after tonight.

The pleasure only lasted for a moment before real life intruded. "No, I'm not."

"You are!" she insisted, her arm around him tightening. "You're wonderful. You're going to do something . . . something real and relevant and meaningful with your life."

"Molly," he said, dropping her eyes. "I haven't even told my brothers yet." He scoffed and it sounded bitter in his ears. "You're the only person I've ever told."

Her fingers under his chin forced his eyes to meet hers. "The hard part was deciding to follow your heart. Your brothers will forgive you."

He shook his head, dislodging her fingers and sitting up straighter. "You don't know that. You don't know how much they love English & Sons."

"I know for sure that they love you more."

The quiet certainty in her voice made his heart swell with affection for her, made him stronger, made him hopeful that he could follow his dream without losing his brothers. She was a miracle of gentleness and wisdom, of courage and heart.

"Molly, I—"

Buzz. Buzzbuzz.

Buzz. Buzzbuzz.

"You're buzzing," she said. "Again."

"How come *you* never buzz?" he asked her.

He meant the words playfully, as a reference to the orgasm she'd denied herself a few minutes ago, so he hoped he hadn't somehow stepped on her toes when her smile faded.

"No one's looking for me," she said quickly, dropping his eyes.

"I was just kidding. I just meant—"

She cut off his words by leaning forward and pressing her lips to his. They were soft and seeking, a little urgent maybe, and he pulled her closer, slipping his tongue between her lips as his blood quickly drained from one head and started filling another.

Buzz. Buzzbuzz.

She drew back, her sweet little smile back in place as she chuckled softly. "I think you should answer it."

Unable to look away from her beautiful, bright eyes, he leaned to the side, wrestling his phone from his back pocket and pressed it to his ear.

"What?" he demanded.

Stratton's voice answered, "You disappeared."

"I'm busy."

"You missed dinner."

"And?"

"Time for Daisy and Fitz to dance. Then cake."

"Nobody will notice if I'm not there."

"Daisy will notice. She wants a picture. With all of us."

Weston grimaced. His new sister-in-law was a baker and they'd all heard from Fitz how important the wedding cake was to her. She'd allowed Weston's mother to choose the invitations and flowers, the menu, the music, the favors . . . just about everything. But the cake? The cake was *all* Daisy, and he needed to be there, nearby and smiling, when it came time for her to cut it.

"Fine," he growled.

"Did Molly leave?"

"Huh?"

"Molly McKenna? The girl who was dancing with J.C.? You almost got into it. I was watching."

Weston felt his face soften. Of course Stratton was watching. Watching and waiting and ready to beat J.C. Rousseau to a pulp if he so much as laid a hand on Weston. Quiet, protective Stratton, the youngest of his older brothers, the most pragmatic, the fixer. Circuits fired in Weston's brain, neurons putting an idea together, his heart gathering courage and refusing to let it slip away. He glanced at Molly's soft red hair against his chest, recalling the admiration in her eyes, the quiet confidence of her faith in him.

"Strat," he said. "I need to talk to you."

"Well, get your ass down here first," said Stratton, adding slyly, "And bring Molly with you."

Chapter 11

On their way back to the ballroom, Weston stopped by a closet in the front hallway and pulled out a folding chair, then led Molly to his table, pushed his chair right up next to Kate's, and shoved the folding chair in the small space he'd created on the other side.

"Everyone?" he said. "This is Molly. She's joining us."

Molly blushed as Weston's four brothers, their dates, Daisy, and his cousin, Kate, looked up at her with nine different smiles ranging from knowing (Daisy) to delighted (Kate) to teasing (Alex) and everything in between.

"Welcome, Molly," said Fitz, raising his eyebrows and winking at her from across the table. He seemed very much like a man who'd been given the inside scoop by his wife.

"Thanks, Fitz," she said.

"I'm Kate," said Weston's cousin, leaning over Weston to take Molly's hand and offer her a wide, warm smile. "He looks much happier now."

Ashamed of herself for ever thinking poorly of Kate, Molly smiled back at the cheerful blonde. "That makes two of us."

Weston slung his arm around Molly's shoulders. "What was the rush, Strat?"

Stratton eyed his little brother from across the table. "What do you need to talk to me about, Wes?"

Weston's face froze for a second, which was just long enough for Alex and Barrett to pick up on the sudden awkwardness that Stratton seemed to miss.

"Yeah, Wes," said Barrett. "What do you need to talk to Stratton about?"

"Leave him alone," chided Emily, giving Weston a sympathetic smile. "Sucks being the youngest, huh, Wes?"

Weston looked at Molly and smiled. "Doesn't have to."

"I'm Jess," said the stunning, raven-haired beauty next to Alex, to Molly's left. "I think you were sitting with my brothers before."

"The Winslow brothers?" asked Molly.

Jessica nodded. "Did they behave?"

Molly grinned. "They were very supportive of Alex's speech."

"Probably because Rousseau was talking smack about me," groused Alex.

Molly felt her cheeks heat up, because he was right. J.C. Rousseau had made a point of telling his sister, Jax, to stay away from Alex. How odd, because with his arm securely around Jessica's shoulders, he didn't look like the type of man who would philander. He looked about one step away from "I do."

"So, Molly, how do you know Weston?" asked Jessica.

"I'm in a community theater group with Daisy," she explained, then twisting her head slightly to catch Weston's eyes, she added, "I only met Weston tonight."

Jessica's eyes widened with surprise. "The plot thickens . . ."

"What does that mean?" asked Molly.

"Nothing. Just . . . I've never seen Weston so . . . I don't know, ga-ga over a girl. He's been chasing you around all night. And unless you got stung by a bee"—Jessica pointed to her own lips with a grin—"he keeps catching you."

Molly chuckled softly. "You're trouble."

"That's what they tell me," said Jessica with a wink.

"*My* trouble," added Alex, whom Molly could have sworn wasn't listening, but had apparently hung on every word.

On the table beside her hand, she felt Weston's phone vibrate, and he picked it up and flipped it over. It briefly occurred to Molly to joke, "Your brothers are all here, so who is it this time?" but she realized it really wasn't any of her business. Weston grimaced as he scrolled down the message, pulling his bottom lip into his mouth before typing a quick response and laying it back on the table, facedown. Before Molly could wonder about it further, the music stopped and the bandleader walked to the front of the stage to adjust the microphone.

"Ladies and gentlemen," he said. "Please raise your glasses and welcome Thomas English, who'd like to say a few words to his son, Fitz, and new daughter-in-law, Daisy."

Everyone faced the stage to listen to the last toast, giving Molly an opportunity to examine them each unobserved.

What would it be like to be part of this clan? she wondered, looking around the table.

The English brothers, with their patrician good looks— all tall, fit, blond, and blue-eyed—were also bright and successful, entrenched in Philadelphia society and old money ways. They were, in every way, exceptional. So, it should have been no surprise that the women they'd each chosen seemed to be exceptional too. Soft, lovely Daisy with her genuine warmth and surprising business sense; Valeria, who seemed so fiery; Emily, who looked to be sensible and kind; and Jessica, who was a beautiful minx. They glanced at each other across the table with economical looks, but Molly sensed that the four women were very good friends, and they understood one another without needing to speak actual words.

Even though Molly had been raised far from the city lights and urban sophistication of the English family, the way they communicated, teased, and bantered felt familiar to her, and while she didn't exactly miss Claire and the twins, she longed for a surrogate family in Philadelphia, yearned for that feeling of belonging. She envied the woman who would eventually take her seat, who would sit next to Weston at all the weddings to come, dance with him, go home with him, sleep in his bed, and return in the morning for a boisterous, teasing brunch. It was forward and ridiculous even to imagine, but something about sitting beside Weston, surrounded by his family, felt like coming home.

Mr. English raised his glass, and everyone at the table reached for the magically full champagne glasses that had been refilled by a whisper-quick cadre of servants while he spoke.

"To my second son, Fitz, and my first daughter, Daisy. May your lives be happy, rich, and full of love. Cheers."

As she sipped, Molly looked across the table at Daisy and Fitz, who stared deeply into each other's eyes before sipping their champagne and kissing. And suddenly the music started playing again, but it was the spare sound of a banjo, guitar, and drums that played the first few bars of a bluesy, folksy song.

Daisy pulled back from Fitz, her face erupting into the most beautiful smile Molly had ever seen.

"Sweet Pea?" she asked him, cocking her head toward the band.

"Of course, Mrs. English. What did you expect?"

"Fitz . . ." she said, her eyes glistening as she shook her head back and forth in pleased surprise.

Fitz stood up, offering his hand to his bride. "Dance with me, wife?"

"Absolutely."

Daisy spared a quick look at the bridal party as she took his hand. "I expect all of you out there in the next two minutes!"

"What do you say?" asked Weston, grinning at Molly with a sparkling, happy gaze.

Out of the corner of her eyes, Molly caught Kate's wistful grin, trained on her cousin and his bride.

"I think you're Kate's escort," she said, softening her refusal with a smile. "I'll wait for you here."

"You're one in a million, Molly McKenna. Save me a dance? I'll be back as soon as we take cake pictures in the dining room."

"I'll be here," she said.

He leaned down and kissed her lips tenderly—which wasn't lost on his remaining three brothers, who whooped softly—before offering his hand to Kate. "Ready to dance, cousin of mine?"

Kate's face brightened and Molly knew she'd done the right thing. As the rest of the brothers led their dates to the dance floor, Molly sat back in her seat, watching, not feeling lonely at all. More and more as the evening progressed, she felt increasingly sure that whatever was happening between her and Weston wasn't going to end tonight. No, he hadn't asked for her number or for a date, but her intuition told her this wasn't a one-night relationship. And no, she didn't know where they'd go from here, exactly, but giving each other a chance beyond tonight felt certain.

Which is why she definitely, positively should have minded her own business . . .

Buzz. Buzzbuzz.

Buzz. Buzzbuzz.

. . . but curiosity got the better of her.

She eyed Weston's phone, shifted her pursed lips back and forth, trying to decide what harm it could do for her to flip it over and see who was trying to get in touch with him. She shouldn't have done it. She had no right. She positioned a clean knife under the phone and with a little flick, it toppled face-up.

The screen was locked, but the latest text was previewed, and she leaned over to read the words.

> CONNIE: You've given me hope. Of course, darling. Tomorrow is perfect. I love you.

Feeling like the wind had just been stolen from her sails, Molly tried to suck in a deep breath, but came up short. She blinked rapidly, looking at the text again, then down at her lap. When she finally managed to fill her lungs, it had the added effect of filling her eyes. Trying to swallow past the lump in her throat, she knew she wasn't going to be able to and it would be best for her to leave.

Weston had his back to her on the dance floor, but Kate was engrossed in conversation with him and wouldn't notice Molly slip out. She grabbed her purse, pushed in her chair, and exited the ballroom via a side door.

The next time Weston spun Kate, he noticed the bridal party table was empty and his chest squeezed for a moment before he told himself not to be an ass. Molly probably went to the bar to get a drink or to the ladies' room, and dancing with Kate instead of Molly gave him a few minutes to process the fact that Connie had texted him about two minutes before his father's speech.

She'd written that she regretted their conversation this morning, loved him, and wished she'd given him a chance to make his case for them giving their relationship a real try.

She wondered if they could talk sometime soon. Anxious to tell Connie that there was no hope for them—to settle things between them once and for all—he told her to call tomorrow. He didn't relish the idea of telling her the ship had sailed, but it had to be done. Though he had no idea how things would play out with Molly, he knew for sure he wasn't, nor would he ever be, in love with Connie.

And yes, he was hoping the only girl in his life, in his bed, in the near future, would be Molly.

"I like your Molly," said Kate.

"She's not mine yet."

Kate shrugged. "It's on."

"You think?"

"Oh, it's on. A hundred percent. Just don't screw it up."

"I'll do my best," he said, sneaking another look at the empty table.

"I'm sorry we keep talking about him, but . . . I just heard that Étienne was in a car accident a few days ago," said Kate softly. "Did you know that? Jessica just told me when we were in the powder room together."

"I considered telling you when we danced before, but I didn't think it was appropriate."

"I don't hate him," said Kate earnestly. "All of you hate him much more than I do."

"Stratton looked ready to strangle J.C. just to hurt Étienne by proxy," said Weston, who wasn't interested in hearing anything remotely good about Étienne Rousseau. "It was a fucked up thing he did to you, Kate, leading you on like that."

"He didn't lead me on. Not really. He never promised me anything, Wes. He was so—" She dropped his eyes, her face soft and wistful, and a little sad, as she sorted through her memories. "You have to understand . . . I thought I loved him. I thought he—well, at the time, I thought he loved me too, so . . ." She was quiet for a moment, but when she looked up again, her expression was crisp. "For him, that was the end of it. For me? I just wasn't ready for all of the feelings that a girl feels when she . . . you know, sleeps with someone for the first time."

"Nice to outgrow that shit show, huh?"

Kate gave him an incredulous grin. "You're kidding, right?"

"No. We're all adults now. We can handle that sort of thing."

"Oh, Weston. You make me want to weep with your ignorance. Girls don't *ever* outgrow that particular shit show. Sleep with us at your peril, because it *always* means more to us than it does to you. The girl who loves casual sex is a myth, a unicorn."

He grinned at his cousin as the song ended, but his stomach turned over uneasily as he realized Molly wasn't back from the bathroom yet. He released Kate, feeling for his phone in his back pocket. Not that Molly had his number, it was just second-nature, but it wasn't there anyway. He gulped as he looked back at the table and saw it sitting in front of Kate's empty chair, face up, screen glowing.

"Hey! Dining room? Cake pictures?" reminded Kate, hooking her thumb toward the dining room, which was the opposite direction than their table, where Weston was heading.

"I'll be right there."

Weston sprinted over to the table, his spirits sinking as he grabbed the phone, which showed a single text on the bright screen. Reading it, he swore softly and he knew: Molly hadn't gone to the bathroom. Molly was just plain gone.

"Shit," he muttered again, tucking his phone into his back pocket and striding across the dance floor to the door that led to the dining room. The photographer had Daisy and Fitz posing as though about to cut the cake and the rest of the bridal party stood nearby watching, waiting to be summoned.

Weston slipped inside the room and pulled the door behind him, sliding one of the twenty-four gilt chairs away from the vast dining room table and slumping down unhappily. Of course she hadn't been able to see Weston's sterile message to Connie that read: *Busy night. Talk tomorrow?* Based on Connie's language—calling him "darling" and saying she loved him—he guessed how Molly had interpreted the message: like he was getting back together with Connie tomorrow. Fuck.

Well, there was nothing he could do about it now. He'd do the pictures for Daisy and go to bed. Before she and Fitz left for their honeymoon, he'd get Molly's phone number and give her a call. Maybe he could explain the context of his messages with Connie, and hopefully Molly would still agree to go out with him.

"Wes."

He looked up to see Stratton pulling out the chair beside him.

"Hey."

"You okay?"

"Not one of my ten best days, Strat." He sighed, finally hitting a wall.

Although meeting Molly had rocked his world, he was pissed with the way things had ended between them tonight. Not to mention, he'd gotten four hours of sleep last night, been broken up with, been forced to attend his brother's wedding stag, met this sexy, angry girl at the bar, almost slept with her, met her again, gotten to know her, almost lost her, almost slept with her, talked—really talked—to her, fallen for her, and lost her again. His energy was sapped. He was exhausted. All he wanted to do was finish the pictures, shove a piece of cake in his mouth, and go to

sleep until tomorrow when he could—maybe, hopefully—
track down Molly.

"You needed to talk to me?"

The interesting thing about hitting a proverbial wall is
that you had nowhere else to go. It was time to stop running.
It was time to tell his brothers the truth.

"I don't want to work for English & Sons," he confessed
wearily.

Stratton's brows creased as he searched Weston's eyes.
"What do you mean?"

He locked his blue eyes with Stratton's, wondering if Molly's sister Claire had red hair and brown eyes and if that had
made it harder for Molly to break the news that she was
leaving Hopeview and moving to Philly.

"I don't want to work for English & Sons. I want to work
for the Philadelphia district attorney's office."

"What are you talking about? Why?"

"I don't want to be a corporate lawyer. I want to defend
kids who make stupid mistakes and ruin their lives." Molly's
voice was so clear in his head, it was like she was whispering
in his ear. "I want to make a difference."

Stratton swallowed, looking disappointed, looking uncomfortable but, amazingly, not abandoning the conversation.

"It's going to be bad when you tell them."

"Bad for who when you tell what?" asked Alex, plopping
down on the arm of Stratton's chair. He ran a hand through
his hair. "I promise you guys when it's Jess's and my turn,
we're not doing four million pictures."

Weston looked at Alex, then back at Stratton, who pursed
his lips and shrugged.

"Hey," said Alex. "Seriously, what's going on here?"

"Is something going on?" asked Barrett, standing in
the V created by Weston and Stratton's chairs, his arms
crossed over his chest.

Alex eyed Stratton, then Weston, warily. His eyes remained on Weston. "I don't know yet."

Weston looked at Stratton again, wishing there was an easier way to do this.

"Wes doesn't want to—"

"I don't want to work for English & Sons."

Barrett's eyes widened and his lips tightened, but he didn't say anything, just stared at Weston like he'd suddenly morphed into an alien life form.

"*What?*" demanded Alex, springing from his perch on Stratton's chair. "What the *fuck* are you talking about?"

"Calm down, Al," said Stratton.

"Fuck you, Strat." Then, to Weston, "What the hell is going on?"

Weston took a deep breath, looking at Barrett again. Letting down Alex and Stratton sucked. Bad. But letting down Barrett, whom Weston had idolized from birth, really and truly ached.

"Try to understand. It's not what I want."

"What *do* you want, Wes?" asked Alex in a clipped tone.

"Just tell them," advised Stratton.

"I want to work for the district attorney's office in the juvenile defense division."

"You want to go into politics?" spat Barrett. "Are you insane?"

"I didn't say I wanted to go into politics," said Weston, keeping his voice calm and even. "I want to defend stupid teenage kids who make one bad—really bad, maybe—mistake and end up paying for it for the rest of their lives."

"Ohhhh," said Alex. "You want to defend criminals instead of taking your rightful place in the family business built by our father and entrusted to—"

Stratton stood, placing a hand on Alex's shoulder, but Alex shrugged him off.

"Stop taking his side, Strat!"

"I'm not," Stratton insisted. "But he has a right to do what he wants to do with his life."

"So, why don't you quit too? And me? And Fitz? And Barrett? And there won't be any more English & Sons! How's that?"

Weston stood up, clenching his jaw as he looked at the hurt and betrayal on Alex's face. "Sorry, Alex, but this isn't personal. I gotta go with my gut. My gut says public defender."

"Your gut says *quitter*," hissed Alex, jabbing his finger in Weston's chest before pivoting sharply and stalking away.

Weston flashed his eyes to Barrett and swallowed the wince he felt, staying as stoic as possible. "It's not personal, Barrett."

"Feels personal, Wes. The idea was always for all us to work together. To build something." Barrett's face was pinched and disappointed as he turned away to follow Alex.

"Stratton?"

Stratton shrugged. "I'll talk to them. When are you talking to Fitz and Dad?"

"Tomorrow."

The weight of Stratton's hand on his shoulder was welcome. "It'll be okay in the end. They're just upset."

"You're not?"

"I get it," he said. "Because I love walking into that office every day. I love the numbers. I love spending the day with Barrett and Fitz, the shorthand of working with Alex, the way Dad pops his head in to get my opinion on a deal. For me, it's a rush. It makes me feel great."

"And that's awesome for *you*, Strat, but I—"

"I didn't finish." Stratton dropped his hand and gave Weston a grim smile. "I can't imagine what it would be like to dread going to work every day, and if working for English

& Sons sounds terrible to you . . . well, you gotta go a different way. I can't say I'm not sorry. But, I get it."

Daisy was calling all of them over to stand in couples behind the cake.

Weston put his hand on Stratton's arm, feeling infinitely grateful for the brother whose quiet ways had always been one of the most comforting forces in Weston's life.

"Thanks, Stratton."

As he walked over to the cake, he looked at Barrett and Alex, who glowered at him from their places on either side of Fitz.

"It'll be okay in the end," Stratton said again, none too convincingly. "Just give it some time."

Chapter 12

"What do *you* think?" Molly asked the chestnut-colored Tennessee Walker. The dark green and gold sign over her immaculate stall read "Biscuit," and the mare had a pretty white patch that ran from her forelock to her muzzle. Molly reached up to stroke her smooth hair and the horse leaned closer. "Oh, you're such a love."

When Molly first left the ballroom, she headed back to the front hall, determined to leave once and for all. But to her left was the parlor where she'd cried about Dusty after Weston's toast, and her confused heart skipped a beat, remembering his arm around her shoulders. Wandering into the snow-lit parlor, she remembered his words, *I follow you willingly every time*. It was probably just her romantic imagination, but as Molly gazed at a portrait of all five brothers hung over the fireplace, Weston's eyes beseeched her to stay.

She wished she hadn't read the text. Most problematic were the words *you've given me hope* because Molly wondered what Weston had said to make Connie feel that way. Had Connie asked for another chance with him and he'd told her "maybe"? It hurt Molly to think so, but it didn't make sense. When she'd told him to dance with Kate, he'd made her promise to wait for him, to save him a dance, and then he'd leaned down to kiss her. Now it's true, Weston could be the black-hearted player of the century, romancing one girl via text and another at his brother's wedding, but Molly had good gut instincts and something told her that she wasn't seeing the whole picture.

Was she ready to leave? No.

Was she ready to give up on Weston? No. No, she wasn't.

Maybe it was ridiculous to even contemplate after a five or six hour acquaintance, but what she realized with searing clarity was her heart had already been compromised. She liked Weston English. She *really* liked him. And yes, she met him at a wedding, and yes, there was a chance he was using her for a good time and she wouldn't hear from him again after tonight. But as the hours strode onward, she had a harder and harder time believing that was true.

I couldn't fall for you this fast if my heart belonged to her.

Molly had left the parlor but headed for the kitchen instead of her car. She waved at the kitchen staff who'd seen her a couple of times now and grabbed a roll from a tray as she passed by, her empty tummy growling. She pulled on Eleanora English's waders and borrowed her red canvas barn jacket, buttoning it up as she made her way out to the stables, hoping that Weston would find her there sooner than later.

And as she and Biscuit had a heart-to-heart, she realized she wasn't getting out of the way for Connie. Molly was only getting out of the way if Weston asked her to.

Biscuit nickered softly and Molly turned from the mare's soft muzzle to the barn door entrance where Weston appeared like magic, snow dusting his hair and his shoulders, twinkling like glitter in the soft night lights of the stable.

"You didn't leave," he said with quiet surprise, standing just inside the door.

Her heart tripped. "Did you want me to?"

His stride across the barn was long and determined as he closed the distance between them and pulled her roughly into his arms.

It was exactly the answer Molly had been hoping for.

Weston closed his eyes, feeling relieved and profoundly grateful for yet another chance with Molly. Her clean Wisteria smell was mixed with snow and straw now—*How long had she been here?*—and he breathed deeply, holding her tightly against him.

After the pictures, Weston had left the dining room without a word, feeling the hot, angry eyes of Barrett and Alex on his back. Photos finished, duty complete, he wouldn't be returning to the wedding again tonight. He went to his room immediately, hoping Molly would suddenly be there as she was last time. When he found the room still and empty, his heart had clutched with disappointment, and he'd had to remind himself that he could ask Daisy for her number tomorrow. *This isn't the end. This isn't the end.*

He sat down on his bed and thought about his brothers' reactions to the news that he wouldn't be joining the firm. Stratton was disappointed, but quietly accepting, anxious to help mend bridges as soon as possible. Barrett was cold and let-down, looking at Weston with disillusionment and regret. But Alex's reaction had been the most fiery, the most blatantly angry. Weston understood. When Alex was faced with the most challenging situation of his life—how to have a life with Jessica away from Philadelphia—he'd never once considered leaving English & Sons, his only goal to make space for both his love and his work in his life. Alex loved Jessica more than English & Sons, but Weston guessed that the margin was narrower than people would guess.

He knew that Fitz's reaction would fall somewhere between Stratton and Barrett's, not quite as accepting, not quite as damning, but also inconvenienced because Fitz would be the only lawyer on staff now. Weston's decision would make more work for Fitz until they hired someone else. He was sorry for that. He was sorry for all of it. But he wasn't sorry for choosing the right path for his life, and his energy and enthusiasm surged as he imagined the kids he'd be defending—maybe some of the kids that left Molly's class showing promise, but fell in with a bad crowd instead. The connection he felt to her as he surveyed his future was strong. If he was honest, her story, commitment, and sacrifices were what had fueled his determination tonight. Molly's example had given him the courage he needed to make the right choices for his life. And he was deeply grateful to her.

But sitting on his bed alone, his chest still felt hollow without her. Angry that Connie's texts had driven Molly away, he fished his phone out of his back pocket and looked at the messages again.

> CONNIE: Wes, I've been wretched since we left each other this morning, you in your handsome tux with those glorious roses, and me pushing you away. You were asking me for a real chance, for a commitment. You wanted to give us a chance, and I stupidly shot you down. I should have said yes, darling. I should have told you that I love you. I should have said that giving us a chance scares me because if I love you and you don't end up loving me back, you'll break my heart. But by turning you away, now I'll never know. Is it too late? Please can we talk, darling? I know you're at Fitz's wedding, but call me as it winds down. Your Con.
>
> WESTON: Busy night. Talk tomorrow?
>
> CONNIE: You've given me hope. Of course, darling. Tomorrow is perfect. I love you.

He hadn't meant to give her hope.

Weston already knew how he felt about Constance—his time with Molly had made his feelings for Con abundantly clear. Tomorrow's conversation would be short and awkward, and probably painful for her. He wasn't interested in pursuing a relationship with Connie . . . the only person he was interested in pursuing was the woman in his arms right now.

"I'm so glad to see you," Weston whispered in her ear. "I thought you'd seen the text from Constance and left."

"I did see it," Molly admitted. "And I did think about leaving."

"Why didn't you?"

"Because I don't know what you said to her."

Weston leaned back, searching her lovely face. "Do you want to know?"

Molly nodded.

"I said four words to her: 'Busy night. Talk tomorrow.'"

"Oh."

He could tell Molly wasn't reassured by this answer. He drew back from her, taking her hand and leading her into one of the empty stalls. It was covered in fresh straw with several bales piled up in the corner. Sitting on one of them, he pulled her down beside him.

"Connie wants to get back together. Or rather, not *back* together, just together . . . um, it'll be easier if I explain my conversation with her this morning."

So he did. Holding hands with Molly, he told her that Connie left for Italy this morning and although he'd asked for a "real chance" with her, when push came to shove, he was unable to tell Connie that he loved her.

"That must have been a difficult conversation," said Molly, her thumb stroking his hand in the most gentle, distracting way, and *Oh, God!* he wanted to be finished discussing Constance so he could concentrate on Molly.

"At the time, it was. But, I was more irritated than sad, to be honest. I mean, I like Connie. I'll always like Connie. And who wants to go to his brother's wedding stag? I was steamed about it, but I have to confess . . . I knew Connie had done me a favor in walking away. I don't love her. I don't want her."

Molly sucked her bottom lip between her teeth, and Weston gasped softly, his eyes drawn to her mouth like a tractor beam.

"Please don't do that again until I finish telling you everything," he begged.

She let go of her lip and her eyes darkened just a touch.

"Anyway, she texted me earlier. She loves me and she was sorry that she shut things down between us this morning, and she wondered if it was too late to give things a chance. She asked if I would call her tonight after the wedding."

"In Italy?"

"It's early morning there."

Molly nodded. "And you replied, 'Busy night. Talk tomorrow.'"

"Yeah." He swallowed. "She poured her heart out. I can't just ignore it. I'll call her in the morning and tell her that . . . that . . ."

Molly turned her face to his, her eyes wide and wondering as she captured his. Her voice was intense—low and soft— when she asked, "What will you tell her?"

"I'll tell her that I met someone at Fitz's wedding. I'll tell her that the girl from the wedding turned my world upside down over the course of a few hours. I'll tell her the thought of not knowing the girl from the wedding after tonight is eating me up from the inside out. I'll tell her there's no room in my heart right now for anyone else except for the girl from the wedding, and I'm so sorry, but I'm just not available anymore."

"Wes . . ."

"Go out to dinner with me tomorrow night."

"Yes."

"And Monday and Tuesday and Wednesday nights too."

She grinned at him, shaking her head, her face bright and delighted. "You'll get sick of me."

"I don't think so. And how about Thursday?"

"Your brother's fiancée, Emily, invited me to go out for drinks."

Weston smiled, chuckling softly. "Of course she did . . . Friday?"

"Rehearsal. With Daisy gone for the next two weeks, I can't miss this one."

"I'll come and take Daisy's place," he said, remembering what his sister-in-law had shared about hanging out with Molly in the backstage darkness. That sounded just about perfect to Weston.

"You're a little crazy," she said, but her eyes were tender.

"About you."

Her smile was priceless and adorable. "You've only known me a handful of minutes!"

He nodded, pulling her closer and dropping his eyes to her lips. "That's true . . . but they've been pretty great minutes. I've got a feeling about you, Molly McKenna, my sweet Samaritan. I get the feeling I'd bend for you."

He watched her eyes dilate to almost black, knowing his were doing the same.

"Let's just start with tomorrow," she whispered, leaning closer to him, reaching up to touch her fingers to his cheek.

"Let's just start with tonight," he countered, tilting his head as it drew closer to her lips.

"Done." She sighed as his lips touched down on hers.

To date, Weston had kissed her gently, hungrily, and frantically. This kiss was different. This kiss was about melting,
savoring, blending, fading into her, into him. As his lips
moved over hers in a deliberate, inevitable ballet, his fingers
skimmed from her shoulders to the front of his mother's red
canvas jacket, opening the buttons one by one, little plucking sounds bringing her closer and closer to feeling his skin
pressed against hers.

Because that's where they were headed. That's definitely
where they were headed. Mouth to mouth. Hand to hand.
Hand to body. Body to body. It's what Molly wanted. It's what
Molly refused to overthink because they'd been teasing each
other with the promise of sex since the moment they met, and
so many hours later, both were starved and exhausted. The
only sustenance would be their joining; the only rest, their
hearts beating in tandem as Weston buried his body in hers.

Molly slipped her hands under the lapels of his jacket,
and he pulled his arms back so it slid down his shoulders,
then she shrugged out of her own, too. The barn was heated,
but cool, and the skin on her bare arms puckered as the
night air kissed her.

Weston found her hands and guided her onto the soft,
thick pile of straw at their feet, half-covering her body
with his as he kissed her with increasing hunger. His lips
were firm and soft, his tongue like wet silk, sliding deca-
dently along hers. His hands unlaced from hers and one
glided up, over her dress, from her hip to her breast, which
he massaged and molded gently. Molly moaned into his
mouth, the growing heat in her core forcing her to fight for
patience. She arched her back and his other hand slipped
under her body to unzip her dress and unclasp her bra.
Molly's eyes were closed, but she felt him hovering over her,

felt his eyes on her face as she sighed with relief, letting her bare back fall onto the bristly but soft straw once again. It heightened the sensitivity of her already aroused skin.

When she opened her eyes, Weston stared at her, his eyes dark blue, his lips glistening from their kisses, his chest heaving. He didn't say anything as his hand released her breast, sliding to her shoulder where he fingered the black strap of her dress before covering it with his palm and dragging both down her arm until half of her chest and one breast was bared to him.

She gasped, feeling the already-hard nipple pebble, fully erect, a tiny spot of bright pink skin that silently begged for his kiss, his hot, wet tongue, and the sensation of lips sucking greedily. She longed for the rush of wet she'd feel between her legs, waiting, waiting, waiting, behind a weak dam ready to break.

"Are you sure you want to keep going?" he asked, his voice gravelly and breathless.

Molly nodded. "I'm sure."

His eyes flashed and his lips tilted up just for a moment, as she imagined they would if they were side by side at the bottom of a rollercoaster about to start its slow ascent to the first drop. She threaded her fingers through his hair and deliberately guided his mouth to her breast.

His tongue made a lazy rotation around the stiff nub of flesh as Molly whimpered greedily, bowing her back to get closer to him. As his lips closed around the sensitive skin, she bucked against him, the dam finally giving way as her panties flooded with wet. He licked and sucked on her tender flesh, finally kissing the very tip of her breast before baring the other and loving her all over again.

Molly's eyes rolled back in her head as his thumb played with her nipple, flicking and rubbing the damp, turgid flesh as his lips and tongue worked relentlessly on its twin.

Her whimpers became louder, small, staccato sounds bonding together into a breathless cry, the heat in her core rising, her hidden muscles bunching tighter and tighter until—

"Weston!" she cried as he brought her to climax. She bucked against him, shuddering and shaking as her insides flexed and relaxed, her bottom lip held tightly between her teeth and her eyes clenched as sharp waves of pleasure peeked then gentled, leaving her limp and loose.

She opened her eyes to find him leaning over her again, and her body, starving for more, pressed up against his. Her fingers moved swiftly to his shirt, and she smoothed her hands over his chest before fingering the buttons, nimbly unfastening them.

"Unzip," she panted, frustrated that she couldn't help him with his shirt and pants at once.

His eyes widened as he moved his hands to his waist, unbuttoning and unzipping as Molly pushed him to his back and straddled his waist, her dress bunched around her hips, her breasts and belly exposed to him.

She ran her hands over the curves of his chest, over his white T-shirt, stopping at the hem to push it up and bare his chest. Her palms skimmed the naked skin and she dropped her gaze from his eyes to watch her hands trail over the ridges and con-tours of muscles, the smooth definition, the light smattering of coiled blond hairs tickling as she explored him. He reached behind his neck and pulled the shirt off, jackknifing his body into a sitting position with Molly still straddling his lap.

She gasped to feel the heat of his chest suddenly pressed intimately into hers. Winding her hands around his neck, her lips slammed into his, teeth clashing, tongues collid-ing, his fingers curling into the skin of her back as she crushed her breasts against him. His rigid erection pushed against her panties through his pants, and her impatience roared to life. She wanted to feel him—all of him—moving on top of her, moving inside of her.

Pressing kisses against his cheek, she burnt a path to his ear, grabbing the lobe of pillowed skin between her teeth and loving his low, guttural groan of pain or pleasure. She panted into his ear, her breath making him shudder against her, making goose bumps rise on his neck under her fingers, as though every part of him was rising and hardening in response to her. She loved it. It made her bold. It made her want more.

She unclasped her hands, sliding them over his shoulders and pushing against his chest to urge him down on the straw. He threw an arm over his eyes like he knew what was coming, and Molly shimmied down his legs, letting her breasts drag over his chest as her lips followed. Kissing his throat and his pecs, his six pronounced abdominal muscles, back and forth, back and forth, to the V of muscle that pointed to her destination.

Slipping her fingers into the waistband of his unzipped pants and boxers beneath, he pushed his pelvis up for a moment so she could tug both down and free him. Rock hard and pointed straight up, Molly reached out to grasp his sex, marveling at the way it felt like velvet-covered steel, veined like a painting, pulsing with life.

"Jesus, Molly. Please. . . ."

His body was on fire, and he was starting to wonder how long he'd be able to hold out if she kept doing what she was doing. It felt so good—so incredible—the way her tongue stroked up and down the length of his erection, but he didn't want to come in her mouth; he wanted them to come together.

"Ahhh," he groaned, a raspy, surprised sound, as she took the head of his cock between her lips, letting her tongue circle the tip as his tongue had circled her nipple. She tongued his length, the contact exhilarating and teasing at once, and then—*Oh God!*—she worked her lips around him until the tip of his cock bumped the back of her throat. Surrounded by slippery, saturated heat, a gathering tightness built in his core, swirling with demands for more, even as his brain warned him to stay in control. He plunged his hands into her hair, letting the silken strands fall through his fingers as she sucked and licked him, pushing him closer and closer to a point of no return.

"Molly . . ." he gasped suddenly, reaching under her shoulders. "Come here."

She looked up at him in surprise. "You don't want—"

"I do want," he panted. "Together."

He sat up, running his hands down to her hips, pushing at the fabric of her dress, her discarded bra, her panties beneath. She knelt on the hay beside him and let him bare her body, holding his eyes as her breasts heaved up and down with the force of her breathing. She stood, letting her dress and panties pool around her feet, looking down in surprise at her boots.

Her eyes were dancing and merry as she looked back at his face.

"What do you think?" she asked, striking a pose, completely naked except for his mother's scuffed, muddy, knee-high, bright red, rubber boots.

He threw an arm under his head and lay back against the hay staring up at her, his erection rock-hard and heavy on his belly, his body tight, taut and expectant, his pants bunched around his knees.

"I've never seen anything so sexy," he answered honestly, grinning back at her.

Damn it, but she made life *fun*. She was sexy as hell, and her eyes twinkled with mischief. He stared at her, growing impossibly harder as his eyes glided from her breasts to her trim waist, to the soft white skin of her belly, to the trim triangle of red curls at the apex of her thighs and her long legs, the entire package dusted with freckles, like angel kisses. He wouldn't have guessed a somewhat-sheltered farmer's daughter would be so comfortable in her own skin, so bold and fearless, striking a pose in a barn while wearing nothing but his mother's old boots. It was so surprising and charming, he felt the slippery slope beneath his feelings for her giving way, marking another moment when he actually *felt* himself falling for her.

Her eyes were dark with desire as he trailed back up her body to find them. She kicked off the boots, and then leaned down to pull off his boots and pants. He lay naked beneath her, looking up and wondering, breathlessly, what was coming next.

Holding his pants in her hand, she stared at his erection for a long moment before licking her lips and cocking her head to the side. "Do you have . . . ?"

"Back left pocket," he answered, and he watched her reach in and pull out his wallet. "Right side."

"Under the Platinum card?" she teased, opening his wallet.

Plucking the foil wrapper from the folds, she tossed his pants and wallet to the side, parting her legs so that her bare feet flanked his thighs. He forgot how to breathe, holding his breath as Molly stood over him in her naked glory, holding a condom between two fingers like an offering.

Her lips tilted up in a smile, but her body was flushed and her breathing was shallow. She wanted him as much as he wanted her.

"Come here," he whispered on a long exhale, sitting up against the bale of hay and holding his hands out to her.

She laced her fingers through them and dropped to her knees on either side of him, resting her pert ass on his thighs. Weston leaned forward to claim her lips, kissing her slowly, longingly, as she untangled their hands and ripped open the condom. As they kissed, she rolled it over his cock then scooted forward so it was pressed against her belly and her breasts rubbed against his chest.

"This has to be a dream," he murmured, pulling away from her, sliding his hands up her back to cup her neck.

"It's not." She was breathing heavily, the hard tips of her nipples razing his skin with each breath. "Remember when you said you were falling for me?"

"I meant it," he said, suddenly reminded of his talk with Kate on the dance floor. "This? Right now? Between us? It's not casual to me, Molly. I don't know where we'll go from here, but I feel like we're at the beginning of something good."

"Me too," she whispered, leaning up on her knees, and reaching down to position his cock at the entrance to her sex. "And I'm falling for you."

With her arms draped loosely around his neck, she held his eyes as she lowered herself slowly, taking his hard thickness, inch by inch, into the tight, wet glove of her body. Swallowing loudly and breathing raggedly, he reached for her hips, careful not to dig his fingers into her soft, warm flesh. Her breasts rose and fell rapidly, pushing against him as she rocked forward, and he gasped as felt himself slip into her to the hilt. With her knees as leverage, she rocked up and then back down again, the walls of her sex clasping his pulsing flesh, massaging it, the gentle, wet friction making him swell inside of her.

"God, Molly. You're . . . You feel so . . ."

"Good," she moaned, closing her eyes and leaning back.

He tightened his arms around her and dipped his head to take one of her nipples between his lips as she moved slowly up and down again. She moaned softly and Weston released her breast to lean forward, holding her back with one arm and cradling her head with the other.

As she lay down, her legs skimmed up his, her ankles crossing over his ass instinctively and allowing him to slide even deeper into her body with an unworldly groan. He cupped her face with his palms, staring into her eyes, which were liquid and dark, as he pulled back and thrust into her again. His feet pushed against the hay bale for leverage and she whimpered, biting her bottom lip as he filled her completely.

"I feel like I'm vibrating," she murmured, her eyes fluttering. And he felt it, too—the flexing and tightening of her muscles around him. Her fingers tensed around his neck, her nails pressing into his skin. "Come with me, Weston."

"I will," he groaned.

He thrust into her again and again, faster now, the pressure building and swirling between his legs, in his stomach, radiating out to his fingertips and toe tips and the very tips of his hair.

"Molly," he panted, his heart pounding as he neared climax, "look at me."

Her eyes opened, drugged and heavy, like a liquid element composed of pure, undiluted lust. She was so beautiful lying beneath him, her body intimately joined with his, trusting and pliant and tender.

"This is just the beginning," he promised her.

Her lips parted and her eyes widened as his mouth dropped to hers and he felt her let go. He swallowed her cries as the walls of her sex convulsed rhythmically around him, sucking, pulling, squeezing, insisting that he join her. His entire body tensed into a tight coil, every muscle taut, his corded arms almost shaking on either side of her head and then . . . and then . . . he threw his head back and cried out her name as he exploded into a blinding climax, surges of pleasure making fireworks burst behind his eyes, and a savage, unstoppable tenderness unfurl in his heart.

Chapter 13

Noticing a thick, wool blanket draped over the stall divider above them, Weston tugged it down and covered them with its warm, scratchy goodness. His hand was soothing in her hair and on her back, sliding up and down her sweat-slickened skin with long, gentle strokes, and Molly snuggled closer to him, her cheek covering his thumping heart and her arm thrown possessively across his chest.

Molly's breathing was slowly returning to normal, but her heart still raced with the magnitude of what they'd just done. Of course Molly had had sex with Dusty, but that was after years of courtship. Molly had been raised a "good girl" by conscientious, church-going parents, and good girls did not generally have hot sex in a barn with men they'd only met a few hours before.

Checking in with her conscience, however, Molly was surprised—but gratified—to discover that she didn't feel any guilt or shame for what she'd just shared with Weston. She didn't know sex could feel like that—a mixture of heat and tenderness, passion and playfulness. She didn't know her body could explode at the same time as her partner's; that had never happened for her and Dusty. In fact, with Dusty, sex was mostly something she did to make him happy, to feel close to him, to let him know she cared about him. For

Molly, it had been less about physical pleasure and more about making an emotional connection. Sex with Weston had been physically mind-blowing in a way she'd never guessed possible, despite the deluge of romance novels she read regularly. But she was in awe of more than just the physical experience of sharing her body with him . . . she'd also felt viscerally, profoundly connected with him, her body to his body, her heart to his heart. She didn't know—*she just didn't know*—that kind of falling-apart and coming-together was possible at the same time.

This is just the beginning.

Oh, God, she thought, *I pray that's true.*

"Are you okay?" Weston asked, pressing his lips to her hair and pulling the blanket more tightly around them before resuming the gentle gliding motion of his hand on her bare back.

"I didn't know," she whispered. "I didn't know it could be like that."

He kissed her head again, then tipped her chin up with his free hand and dropped his lips to hers. A light touch. A caress. It made her stomach flutter with longing. *More.* She already wanted more.

Cupping her cheek to press her head gently back against his chest, one hand skated up and down her back while he laced his fingers through hers with the other.

"Want to know the truth?"

"Yeah."

"Me neither," he said softly.

"What do you mean?" she asked.

"I've been with other women. I was pretty sure I was in love a couple of times too. But, the heat we have? It's like you were made for me. I've never felt anything like it before. I could live inside of your body."

Her lips twitched in satisfaction. "*That* good?"

"Almost scary-good."

"Hush," she protested. "Not scary. Just me."

"You're a phenomenon. Believe me."

"I'm just Molly McKenna," she said.

"No 'just' about it. When I say that you rocked my world, I literally mean that my life as I know it right this minute is completely different than it was before I met you at five o'clock toni—last night."

"Last night?"

"It's after midnight," he said. "And do you know why that's awesome?"

"Tell me," she said, her heart swelling with happiness.

"Because it means that I am starting and ending today with you."

"Cocky!" She laughed softly, leaning on his chest to catch his eyes. "Pretty sure you'll be with me at 11:59 tonight, huh?"

He grinned at her, and she realized he was blushing, which was so adorable, the fluttering in her stomach moved lower, contracting her recently spent muscles, telling her she was almost ready for him again.

"Hoping?" he amended.

She giggled, leaning forward to kiss him.

He kissed her back, tenderly, lovingly, like he was as starving for her as she was for him, like they hadn't just climaxed in each other's arms ten minutes before. Rolling her onto her back, she felt him hardening against her thigh and a thrill cut through her body.

"Do you want to . . . again?" he asked.

"Do you have another condom?"

He shook his head. "Not with me. I didn't count on you, Molly."

She grimaced, thinking of Dusty with Shana. "We can't."

"You're not on the pill? Because I'm careful," he assured her. "I always use protection."

"Except now," she said, sarcastically, raising an eyebrow.

He sighed, nodding. "Except now."

If this truly was the beginning between her and Weston, she'd have time later to tell him about Dusty and Shana. She'd have time to get a clean bill of health before sharing her whole self with him and if he cared for her, he would wait. He would understand.

His lips brushed softly against hers, but she kept her lips together, refusing to be seduced. When he leaned back she offered him a small, chiding smile. "We can't."

"You're a cruel woman, Molly McKenna." He took a deep breath and sighed, rolling off her body onto his back.

She leaned on her elbow, gazing at him, the words tumbling out of her mouth before she could stop them. "Dusty got Shana pregnant . . . while he was still with me."

He turned to face her, his eyebrows furrowing as his face contorted into a sneer. "What a piece of shit."

"And since I only found out last night, I haven't had time to—"

"To get tested," he finished for her, leaning on his elbow to mirror her. "I'm so sorry."

"Presumably she's been to an obstetrician, who would have already tested her for STDs, but I won't feel certain until I've seen a doctor."

Weston reached out, throwing an arm around her waist and pulling her close until her breasts were flush against his chest and their noses touched lightly. She wove her legs between his and he leaned forward to kiss her gently.

"I better not ever meet him, Molly. I wouldn't trust myself not to do some serious damage."

"Good thing it's not a very likely scenario." Molly cupped his cheek and kissed him again. "I wouldn't want that, though, Wes. I don't love him. I don't even like him. I wouldn't want you fighting over me. It wouldn't be worth it."

"It would to me."

"You remind me of my brothers. Overprotective."

"Ah, good. They all live in the same town, right? I'll rest easy knowing that Dusty's going to get what's coming to him." He glanced down at their naked bodies wrapped around each other. "And, ah-hem, I hope I don't remind you of them *too* much."

She cringed, wrinkling her nose. "You're disgusting."

His smile, followed by a spot-on Beavis & Butthead chuckle, was so boyish and silly, she couldn't help but smile back, shaking her head at his antics.

"Hey," he said, his smile fading, "Speaking of brothers, I didn't tell you before, but I spilled the beans. About my plans for the future . . . about working for the DA's office."

"What? You did? When?"

"Tonight," he said, pulling the goodness that was Molly as close to him as possible.

He half-considered getting dressed and running back to the house for another condom, but the reality was that lying naked next to Molly, her soft body pressed up against the hard ridges of his, talking to her, telling her things, was its own version of amazing that he was loathe to part with, even for more breathtaking sex. And that in and of itself said more about what was transpiring in his heart than anything else. Just being with Molly McKenna was enough for now. Especially since he would be buying and bringing a double-sized box of condoms for their date tonight.

"While Daisy and Fitz were having pictures taken with the cake, I told Stratton, but Alex and Barrett overheard."

"And?"

He grimaced. "It didn't go well. They were pissed."

"I'm sorry," she said gently, her face falling with compassion. "When I told my family about coming to Philly to teach, they were furious. My brothers left the room, mumbling about foolish women and big cities. My father looked at me with confused, disappointed eyes before following them out to the barn. But my mother and sister were the worst."

"Why?"

She shrugged, her face taking on a far-away look. "We spent so much time together—like the three musketeers. Baking for the church and school events, making meals, all three of us pitching in to help with the chores throughout my childhood. Claire was married last year, but she and her husband live just up the road from my folks, so we still ate dinner together four or five times a week. It was a blow to them . . ."

Her voice was soft as her words trailed off, and Weston reached forward to brush her hair off her face, gently tucking the strands behind her ear. "It was brave."

She shook her head. "I can't see it like that. It didn't feel like bravery because I wanted it so much. In fact, it was almost selfish. I didn't really even consider my family, or . . . or Dusty." She scoffed, lightly, her eyes wistful. "I was ruined the first time I saw the movie *Stand and Deliver*, I think. I knew what I wanted to do."

"You're the only person I know who'd give up their comfortable life in small-town Ohio, move to a big city where you know no one, go to a bad area of town every day to teach marginalized kids, and call yourself selfish." He kissed her nose then nuzzled it with his. "And *Stand and Deliver* is a great movie."

"Tell me more . . . about your brothers."

He sighed, rolling onto his back, and rubbing his eyes before pillowing his elbows behind his head. "Alex was

furious. Barrett was disappointed. Stratton was . . . helpful.
Fitz isn't going to be happy."

"What about your Dad?"

Weston shrugged, suddenly feeling tired, and though
he didn't second-guess his decision, a little alone. "I don't
know. I'll find out tomorrow."

He didn't expect for Molly to suddenly straddle his waist,
her naked body perched on top of his chest, her brown eyes
serious and tender as they gazed down at him.

"Do I have your attention?" she asked.

His cock twitched, blood coursing like liquid fire through
his veins, hardening it in an instant. He reached for her hips,
kneading the soft warm skin, watching with awe as her bright
pink nipples stiffened to delectable little peaks above him.
Maybe they couldn't have sex again right this minute, but he
knew for a fact he wasn't done enjoying Molly's body tonight.

Her light chuckle distracted him, and he raised his eyes
to hers.

"I have something to say," she said, grinning. "Are you
listening?"

"It's safe to say that there isn't anyone or anything else in
the world that has my attention right this minute, Molly."

Her lips parted and her eyes, languid with longing and
arousal, darkened to black as she stared down at him. His
thumbs slipped down the creases of her thighs, parting
her silken folds. She was wet. No. Soaked. One thumb
held her lips open while the other caressed her gently,
swiping, flicking, priming her with teasing strokes while
he watched her eyes widen and flutter. A little whimper
escaped from her throat and Weston licked his lips. He
knew exactly what he was going to do to her as soon as she
said what she wanted to say.

"I'm listening," he said, his voice low and slow, just short
of breathless.

"I'm . . ." she gasped lightly as his thumb circled the tender nub again. "I'm proud of you. I'm . . . I'm just so . . . proud of . . . you."

And just like that, he wasn't alone anymore. He had Molly on his side, and as long as he had her, he felt like he could do anything.

Brimming with emotion, Weston sat up, putting his arms around her and lowering her gently to the straw. He knelt between her legs and gently draped her knees over his shoulders. Then he leaned forward and let his tongue finish the job his thumbs had started.

"Molly," he whispered, "are you asleep?"

"Not yet," she murmured, her limbs like jelly, her heart slowing down.

After he'd brought her to an earth-shattering climax, he'd gathered her into his arms—her back to his front—piled some hay beneath their heads and pulled the blanket over their shoulders. Spooning beside him, his warm body pressed intimately against hers, the iron band of his muscular arm holding her tight, Molly was completely comfortable and ready to surrender to a few hours of sleep.

"Thank you," he said softly, his breath near her ear.

"For what?" she asked, draping her arm over his, covering his hand with hers.

"For everything. For making the wedding not horrible. For encouraging me to follow my dreams, for not leaving, for . . . this." His took a deep breath, his chest pushing into her back as she stroked his hand lovingly before threading her fingers through his. His voice was soft and tentative when he spoke again. "If you . . . I mean, if you change your mind about us in the morning, I just wanted you to know . . . this was the best night of my life. I wanted to be sure I said that."

Her eyes welled with tears and she released his hand so she could roll over and face him. He tightened his arm around her, his face uncertain, searching her eyes in the dim light.

"Weston," she whispered, touching her lips to his before drawing back. "I won't change my mind."

She didn't realize he'd been holding his breath until he exhaled, the warmth of it soft on her cheek. He leaned forward and pressed his forehead to hers, nuzzling her nose with his, their chests pressed together, her sex and thighs flush against his, their legs and feet entwined.

This, she thought, *is what heaven must feel like.*

"Goodnight, Molly McKenna," he whispered, closing his eyes.

"Goodnight, Weston English," she said, taking one last look before closing her own.

And in the wee hours of the morning, heart to heart and tangled up in each other's arms, they finally fell asleep.

Chapter 14

For the past hour, Weston had been watching Molly sleep.

Her freckles were scattered across her face like stars, in all different tones of brown: warm, light brown; chocolate brown; and there were some, most compelling to him, that were a gentle reddish-tan like her hair. Most heavily concentrated on her nose and cheekbones, he couldn't possibly count them all, but as streams of morning sunshine dappled her skin, he tried. His eyes were drawn to the darker flecks—the one on the thin skin under her eye, another perched on the apple of her cheek, another just grazing her hairline near her ear. These were tiny parts of the woman he'd spent the night with, shared his body with, whom he was reluctant to wake up because the romance-by-proxy of the wedding was over, and he didn't know how they would fit into one another's realities.

He rested his head on the curve of his elbow, marveling at the reddish-brown lashes that lay so softly against her skin. Her lips beckoned him, the lower one more pillowed than the top. He knew what it felt like to have those lips moving beneath his, sliding across his hot skin, the warmth and firmness of them around his sex. He might have sighed longingly as he leaned forward and grazed her lips with his, breathing in deeply, memorizing everything he could about the woman in his arms, just in case, just in case . . .

"Molly," he whispered. "It's time to wake up."

"Mmm," she murmured, curling her body into his and burrowing her head under his chin. She exhaled, her breath hot and damp on the hollow at the base of his throat.

His body, which had been behaving itself since waking up, stirred to life, his blood coursing unerringly to his hips, to his sex, which swelled against her belly.

"Molly," he said again, his voice more gravelly now. "It's morning."

"Mm-hm. Morning." She sighed. She pursed her lips and kissed his neck, then rested them there, pressed against him.

"Molly," he tried again, knowing they needed to get dressed before the stable staff arrived around nine, before he flipped her over and took her again, clean bill of health or not. "It's time for breakfast."

"Ohhhh . . ." Her eyes finally fluttered a little. "Breakfast?"

He grinned. They'd barely eaten a bite last night. She had to be as starving as he was.

"My mom said the caterers would lay out a brunch starting at nine and it's eight forty-five now. You hungry?"

"You're inviting me to breakfast?" she asked, leaning back. Her drowsy eyes were opened but heavy, her face still slack and lazy from sleep. Red, wavy hair tumbled around her neck and shoulders in lovely, messy waves.

"Of course," he replied.

"With your family? They'll know we . . ."

"Does that bother you?"

"Only if . . ." She pulled her bottom lip into her mouth as her voice trailed off, her eyes troubled.

"Only if what, sweetheart?"

Her eyebrows furrowed together briefly as she searched his face. "Only if I was a one-night stand. It would bother me if they thought that."

He leaned forward and pressed his lips to hers. "Then you have nothing to worry about. I'm picking you up tonight at six."

She smiled at him, and it was like the sun had come out; she looked so happy and relieved. "About that . . . would you mind staying in?"

"Not at all."

"Take-out and a movie?" she suggested, her eyes twinkling.

"*Stand and Deliver*?" he suggested. "Your bed or mine?"

She laughed softly, shaking her head like he was being naughty. "My *apartment*. We'll see about my bed . . ."

"We'll see it, alright."

"Hey . . ." Her smile faltered a little and she gave him an uncertain look. "You're not just coming over for *that*, are you?"

"*That*," he said, "as I recall, was mind-blowing. So, I'd be lying if I said I wasn't hoping for a repeat performance. But—"

"But?"

"I'd watch a hundred movies with you if that's what it took for you to feel comfortable enough to invite me into your bed. And I'd be happy just to be with you, Molly."

Her mouth dropped open softly. Her eyes darkened. Her breathing hitched. He heard it happen, and it did crazy things to his chest, which swelled and fluttered like he was a teenager with his first crush.

"Weston?"

"Yeah?"

"You are *so* getting laid tonight."

His sudden laugh was so loud, Biscuit nickered in the stall beside them, and Weston knew—no matter what—he was going to fall in love with this girl. His heart was going to be served to her on a platter to do with whatever she pleased, and he was going to have no say in the matter. He knew it. He felt it. He was fine with it.

Because, hell . . . it was already happening.

As they walked side-by-side, holding hands out of the barn into the morning sunshine back to the main house, Molly realized it had snowed again, and the whole world was covered in a diamond-like frost that glistened and twinkled in the sun. It felt like everything around her reflected the feelings of her heart—bright and hopeful and beautifully alive. How was it possible that she'd woken up almost twenty-four hours ago with red, weepy eyes and a trounced heart, only to find herself so blissfully besotted now? She wasn't sure how it had happened, but her feelings wouldn't be denied. She was falling fast and hard for Weston.

"It's so beautiful this morning." She sighed, tightening her grip on his hand as they drew closer to the house.

"It's got nothing on you," he teased, stopping to lean down and press his lips to her nose. He pulled a piece of straw from her hair. "But you smell like horses."

"You do too," she said, grinning.

"They're going to tease us," he cautioned.

"Good thing I'm the youngest of four," she replied, winking at him. "With twin brothers."

"Try four, all older."

"If you ever meet Trav and Todd," she said, remembering the merciless pranks and teasing she endured at her older brothers' hands, "you'll understand why your four equal my two."

He pulled her into the mudroom and she sat down on the white bench. As he already had several times before, Weston dropped to his knees and helped her take off the boots, then reached behind him for her strappy heels and buckled them in place. Molly's cheeks flushed as she remembered the first time he'd unbuckled her shoes, how she'd ended up in his bed, almost naked, on her back, ready to have cheap, meaningless sex with him.

Thank God Alex had interrupted them. Thank God they'd managed to somehow find their way to something deeper.

"What are you thinking about?" he asked, his voice low, his eyes bright blue and focused as they stared up at her.

"This is the third time you've helped me with my shoes."

"Well, when we met, you said I was the fairytale king, right? From *Cinderella*?"

"You're mixing up your fairy tales," she giggled. "You're thinking of *Sleeping Beauty*."

He shook his head, chuckling softly. "Yeah. But I'm still the fairytale king. I woke up next to you, Beauty."

She leaned forward and put her palms on his cold cheeks, pulling his face to hers and dropping her lips to his. She kissed him gently and tenderly, wanting him to know how much the hours she'd spent with him meant to her, how much she hoped his words from last night—*This is just the beginning*—were the truth.

When she drew back, his eyes opened slowly and he looked taken aback, almost helpless. "What was that for?"

"For making this the best wedding ever."

He grinned at her, standing to shrug out of his coat. She stood and took hers off too, strangely sad to say good-bye to the red canvas jacket that almost felt like hers now.

Buzz. Buzzbuzz.

Buzz. Buzzbuzz.

Molly looked at Weston, but she quickly realized that for the first time the phone in question wasn't his, but hers. It was buzzing inside her purse.

Weston looked at her with laughter in his eyes. "I knew you'd buzz sooner or later."

Molly fumbled with her purse and withdrew the phone, her smile fading as she realized that in addition to a number of unread texts from Dusty, there was now several voice messages, the most recent one just delivered. This was getting ridiculous. As soon as she got home, she'd call Dusty back, tell him to stop bothering her and to never, ever bother her again. He wasn't getting her forgiveness, but she was moving on and there was no room for him in her future.

"Bad news?"

Molly looked at Weston's concerned eyes and felt her face relax and eyes soften as she considered the fact that she had plenty of room for *him* and wanted—more than anything—for Weston to figure prominently in her future.

"No," she said, shaking her hand and gazing at him with all the tenderness in her heart. "Nothing's wrong. Everything's right."

"Ready for breakfast?" he asked, grinning as he offered her his hand.

"As ready as I'll ever be," she answered, holding her head high as she let him lead the way.

Barrett, Emily, Alex, Jessica, Stratton, Valeria, and Kate were already in the dining room when they arrived. Stratton was at the buffet, piling scrambled eggs, bacon, French toast, and fruit on his plate. Barrett and Alex chatted intensely by the coffee. Kate sat at the table, looking less hungover than Valeria, but slightly more than Jessica, who propped up her head on her hand, a mug of steaming coffee before her.

Emily rose to greet them as they walked in.

"We wondered where you two had gotten off to last night."

"Stables," said Stratton, sniffing as he passed behind them to take a seat beside Valeria at the table.

Emily raised her eyebrows at Stratton's back before grinning at Weston and leaning forward to speak in a soft voice. "Barrett's calmed down a little, but I can't speak for Alex. He kept Jess up half the night and not for the usual reasons."

Weston darted a glance at Alex, who'd stopped his conversation with Barrett to stare at Weston with menace. Weston looked down at Molly. "Grab a plate. I'll get you some coffee."

Pressing a kiss to the side of her head before releasing her hand, he was grateful when Emily ushered her over to the buffet. Weston rounded the table and approached his brothers. They parted from in front of the coffee so he could grab two mugs.

"Good morning," said Barrett.

Weston took a deep breath and looked up at Barrett. Emily was right. Barrett was still angry, but his eyes were much softer than they'd been last night, like he was trying to understand, trying to make room for Weston's decision.

"Good morning," he answered.

"Is it?" sneered Alex. "Is it *good*? Because it doesn't feel like *good* to me. It still feels like *disappointment* and *betrayal*."

Weston shifted his glance from Barrett's blue eyes to Alex's, which were narrowed, his lips pursed and puckered.

"I'm sorry you feel that way," said Weston. "But it's my life. I have a right to choose a different path, Al."

"Well, don't expect us to save a position for you. Don't expect to come sailing into English & Sons looking for a job when some clock-in, clock-out, paper-pusher job at the DA's office turns out to be shit."

Weston held Alex's eyes for a long time, feeling anger surge inside of him, but forcing himself to be calm. "You're an asshole, Alex. Just because we shared the same womb and have the same last name, you don't own me. You don't get to choose the direction of my life."

Weston felt a heavy hand on his shoulder and assumed it was Stratton. "Leave it, Strat!"

"Stratton's having his breakfast, son," said the low, familiar voice of Tom English, Weston's father.

Weston whipped his head around with wild, sorry eyes to look at his father. Damn it, but this is not how he wanted his father to find out. He winced. "Dad . . ."

"What? You don't think these two were ranting and raving until two in the morning? I already know, Wes." He dropped his hand from Weston's shoulder. "Can't say I'm not sorry."

"Me too," said Weston, turning his back to his brothers to face his father. "I respect the work you all do at English & Sons. So much. I'm grateful for the life it's afforded me. But . . . but I . . ."

His voice trailed off and he swallowed, feeling a little lost as he tried to explain his life's dream to his father. Glancing over his father's shoulders, his eyes mercifully slammed into Molly's. She stood in front of the buffet, holding a plate, her brown eyes focused on him. In her gaze, he read compassion and pride and . . . and love. Holding his breath as he held her eyes, and filled to the brim with gratitude for her presence and faith in him, he saw everything he needed to give him the courage to finish saying his piece.

Shifting his glance back to his father, he exhaled. "I want to make a difference. I want to defend kids who make crappy choices and push themselves to the brink of ruining their lives. I want to be the one thing that stands between them and a life in the system, in juvenile detention, in jail. I want to understand why they made the choices that led to their arrest and I want to help reverse the direction of their lives." He paused, looking for some indication of his father's thoughts, but his eyes were cool and thoughtful. "I'm sorry. I don't mean to turn my back on English & Sons, Dad, but this is something I have to do."

His father took a deep breath, nodding as he searched Weston's face. "Well, then, I need to tell you that—"

They were all distracted by a sudden ruckus in the front foyer. The sound of a door slamming, feet running, another door slamming, more running feet, getting closer.

"Molly?" a male voice yelled, echoing through the marble halls. "Molly?! Where are you? *MOLLY*?"

Suddenly, the double doors of the dining room burst open, and an enormous man stood—arms stretched, eyes wild—in the doorway.

"Molly!" he cried, zeroing in on her shocked face as he strode across the room to stand before her. "Thank God I found you!"

Molly felt the plate slipping from her hands and would be eternally grateful for Emily Edwards's quick reflexes. When she was able to form words again, she'd need to remember to thank her new friend for catching it.

How the hell an unshaven, rumpled, wild-eyed Dusty Hicks had suddenly appeared in the dining room of the English family's mansion the day after Daisy's wedding was a question that seemed so absurd, she started laughing. Staring at Dusty's face in shock, she felt the giggles start deep in her belly, making shoulders shudder as her eyes suddenly burned with embarrassment and her fists curled in fury.

She felt an arm—a strong, possessive, stable-smelling arm—slip around her waist and she stopped laughing immediately and blinked, looking up at Weston English as a flood of tears welled in her eyes.

"Molly," murmured Weston, concern etched into his handsome face.

With her brain on overload, she tried to speak, but couldn't. Her mouth opened, then closed quickly as Dusty demanded her attention and she jerked her neck to face him.

"Mol . . ." asked Dusty in his loudest, most belligerent voice, "who the *hell* is *this*?"

Emily Edwards's father, Felix, the Englishes' gardener, suddenly appeared in the dining room doorway, huffing and puffing beside a confused butler.

"He . . . jumped . . . the wall. Left his car . . . by the gate-house and . . . jumped the wall!" panted Felix. "I ch-chased him up to the . . . house."

Emily quickly set Molly's plate down on the table and rushed to her elderly father's side. "Daddy, come sit."

Molly's cheeks flamed red as she watched Emily help her father to a seat at the table.

"Sir," said the butler, directing a haughty glance at Dusty. "The family is not receiving guests this morning."

Dusty narrowed his eyes at the butler before jabbing a finger in Molly's direction. "I'm not here for the family. I'm here for *her*."

Weston's fingers curled painfully into her waist, and Molly covered them with her hand, peeling them away gently.

"That's right," drawled Dusty, sauntering a couple of steps closer to Molly. His wide expanse of muscled chest rose and fell rapidly under his rumpled, untucked flannel shirt. "Hands off my girl."

"*Your* girl?" spat Weston.

"Last I checked." Dusty dropped Weston's eyes, sliding his gaze to Molly. "Baby, I know you're mad and that's why you didn't answer my texts, but we need to talk."

"He's been texting you?" asked Weston.

"All night long," purred Dusty. "And Molly played hard-to-get so I'd have to come here in person."

"I never read one text," said Molly, looking up at Weston. "Not one. I deleted them all."

Weston gave her a thin smile, which gave her the courage to let go of her shock and embarrassment and face Dusty with steel in her voice. "I deleted them because there's nothing to say, Dusty."

"Baby, there's lots to say."

"Like what?"

"You want to talk in front of all these people?" he asked in a silky, teasing voice better suited to the bedroom than an audience of English brothers, their fiancées and girlfriends, two fathers, and a butler.

"I don't want—"

"Fine, baby." He shrugged. "Here goes . . . Shana ain't pregnant. I love you. I want you back."

The world spun and Molly's knees buckled, but Weston's arm snaked around her waist again, pulling her against his body. At the same time, Dusty reached for her hand, but she slapped it away.

"Don't touch me," she whispered, testing her legs, grateful that they held.

"Aw, Mol . . . it was just a danged lie she made up. Something about you breaking her brother Joel's heart in the eighth grade. She always wanted to get back at you for it. Said she just wanted to break us up, not get married."

Molly had a quick mental flashback to creepy Joel Evans asking her to the eighth grade formal and swallowed hard.

"Well, she got her wish," said Molly in a breathless voice, grateful for Weston's support, but finally feeling strong enough to stand on her own and face Dusty. She took a step forward, getting ready to tell him off. "We are definitely broken up."

"Come on. We were together a long time, baby. I want another chance."

"Another *chance*?" she asked, followed by another bout of near-maniacal laughter. Weston reached for her, but she lurched away this time. It was too easy to lean on him, and she needed to face Dusty on her own, as Weston had faced his father on his own a few minutes before. She could feel his strength and presence beside her, and she was grateful for his support, but this was *her* fight.

"You're crazy as the loon, Dusty Hicks."

Dusty took a step closer, offering his best smile—the one that had made Molly say yes so many times when she should have said no.

"Baby, look at me. I just made a mistake. You're so sweet and good, Mol. You're the one I love. You're the one I want."

Beside her, Weston cracked his knuckles, and she caught sight of his fingers curling into fists from the corner of her eye. She didn't want a fight. No. Absolutely not. She needed to get Dusty out of here. She'd take him back to her apartment, give him back the ring, and tell him to go home to Ohio.

"Dusty, we'll go talk at my place. Wait for me outside. I'll be there in a minute."

"Sounds good to me," he said, his tone victorious.

Felix stood to escort Dusty back to the front gate and Molly turned to Weston. The confusion and pain in his eyes made her breath catch. "Wes, I just need to—"

He pursed his lips together and nodded. "Yeah, I get it."

"No, I don't think you do, but he drove all the way here and I—"

"I understand," said Weston, though it was clear from his clenched jaw and the hurt in his eyes that he didn't.

"Wes, last night was—"

"You know what I just thought of, baby?" asked Dusty, turning around at the dining room doors to interrupt them.

"Even if you screwed this guy, it's okay by me, because I figure that'll just make us even."

Molly heard several light gasps as she spun with fury to face Dusty and tell him that there was no scenario on earth in which they'd be even. But Weston was faster than she was. In three—two?—strides, he'd crossed the dining room and slammed his fist into Dusty's face. Molly watched in horror as Dusty's nose exploded in a flash of bright red before he faltered backward into one of the two doors. Weston was on him again in an instant with another punch to the jaw and another to the gut.

"You. Don't. Talk. To. Her. Like. That!"

Molly's eyes were round and wild, her hands covering her mouth in horror as Barrett and Alex rushed forward to pull their brother off of Dusty. Thus restrained, Dusty was able to crawl up off the floor, draw back, and get one good hit to Weston's vulnerable stomach. As Barrett continued to pull Weston away, Alex hit Dusty once more in the face, splitting his lip as Dusty fell against the door, slumping to the floor.

"You hit my kid brother!" Alex bellowed, shaking out his fist and climbing over Dusty's body to pull a worried Jessica against his side.

Molly could barely draw a full breath and tears streaked down her cheeks as she looked around the room at the shocked and upset faces, more and more eyes turning to her.

"I'm so . . . I'm so terribly . . ." Her breath hitched as she looked at Weston's face, which was a mask of pain—both from his perception that she *wanted* to spend time with Dusty and from the blow he took to the stomach. She gasped softly, pushing away a new stream of tears. "Weston, I'm so . . ."

He dropped her eyes, looking down quickly, as though the sight of her was unbearable to him. Her chest tightened and she inhaled an audibly ragged breath.

"Mr. English, I'm so sorry," she said to Weston's father, who gave her a pained look and nodded.

Keeping her head down, she stepped over to the dining room door, and with Felix Edwards's help, she lifted Dusty Hicks off the parquet floor and escorted him back out the front door.

Chapter 15

"What the *fuck*?" demanded Alex, still holding Jessica close as he opened and closed his hand to flex his bruised knuckles.

Weston shrugged Barrett's arm from around his shoulder, looking at his older brother with venom. "Thanks so much for helping him get that hit in, Bar."

"I was trying to help, Wes. You'd already gotten him three or four times. You needed to stop."

"Well, thanks again. It felt great." Weston rubbed his aching stomach and looked around at the shocked faces of his family members. "Show's over, everyone. Go back to breakfast."

He didn't trust his emotions, so he was unable to look his brothers, their girlfriends, or his father as he turned and left the dining room. Heading quickly up the stairs, he tried to ignore the ache in his heart that was far more painful than the punch to his abdomen. She'd left with her fiancé. After everything they'd shared last night and this morning, her sleezeball, scumbag ex showed up and within five minutes, she was gone.

Some part of him knew that that assessment was unfair and unkind—what else was she supposed to do? Have a huge fight with her ex-fiancé in front of virtual strangers?—but he couldn't help it. Watching her walk away hurt. It just did.

Weston stripped out of his tux, hidden bits of hay scattering across his bedroom floor as he walked into his bathroom and turned on the shower. Stepping into the warmth, he leaned his forehead against the tile, clenching his jaw as the image of Molly reaching down to help Dusty ran through his head on a loop. What if they got back to her place and Dusty managed—with his "babys" and "I love yous"—to coax her back into his arms? She and Weston hadn't really promised each other anything. Their entire relationship hinged on a date tonight that he didn't feel so certain of anymore. She'd programmed her address into his phone, but should he go over there tonight? God, what if she and Dusty had reconciled by then and Weston walked in on them—

He pounded the wall with his fist, turning around to let the hot water beat down on his back and savoring the sharpness. He was angry with himself too . . . why had he gotten so defensive? Why hadn't he let her tell him whatever she was trying to say? She said, *I just need to* . . . To what? he wondered. What did she "just" need to do with her cheating jackass of a fiancé? Because that guy didn't deserve an ounce of sweet Molly's time. Not a minute. Not a second. And yet . . . there was nothing Weston could do about it right now. It was threatening to eat him alive, but there was nothing to be done.

He had one choice to make: go to Molly's at six o'clock, or not. And he had a whole day before him to figure it out.

In the meantime, before her fuckhead fiancé—*ex-fiancé, Wes. EX*, he reminded himself—broke up their brunch, his father was about to tell him something that had seemed important. He turned his mind to his father and brothers, which, frankly, wasn't a whole lot better than thinking about Molly. Yes, Barrett seemed to have softened, but Alex . . . Alex was still pissed. Except, Weston remembered, his lips twitching, Alex had taken down Dusty with one right hook after that sucker punch. It comforted Weston—hugely— that Alex had shown that kind of instant loyalty and protectiveness. Alex was pissed, yes. But he would come around. Even Weston's father, with his inscrutable poker face, hadn't seemed furious. A little disappointed, maybe, but resigned too. And something else . . .

As Weston toweled off and pulled on some jeans and a T-shirt, he realized he recognized the expression on his father's face. It was the same one they all got when they figured out the answer to a complex situation or troubling problem. He knew what it meant: his father had a solution to Weston's decision not to work for English & Sons, and if his dad's face was any indication, it was a good solution.

Running a brush through his damp hair, he tugged on some leather slippers and headed back downstairs.

Molly barely said a word to Dusty as he drove them back to her apartment in his pickup. At some point it had occurred to her that leaving her car at Haverford Park meant she'd have to go back for it later, but maybe that was part of her design. It gave her a bona fide reason to return. Her stomach flipped over when she recalled Weston's face— he'd looked so betrayed, so hurt. When they stopped at a red light, Molly reached back and slapped Dusty's face as hard as she could.

"Goddamn, Molly! What the hell was that for?"

"For punching Wes!"

"Did you miss the part where he hit me four times first?"

"You deserved it, Dusty. And more."

He rubbed his cheek as he glanced over at her. She felt his gaze on her kiss-swollen lips and tousled hair. "But I wasn't wrong, was I? About you sleeping with him?"

"It's green," she said, her cheeks flushing. "And it's none of your business."

He shook his head. "I can't believe you slept with him . . . I mean, we're hardly broken up."

"Wrong, Dusty. We are totally and completely broken up." She took a deep breath and sighed. "My road's the next up on the left."

"Molly," he said softly. "I meant what I said. I love you. I made a mistake. How do I get a second chance?"

"You don't."

"Why n—"

"Dusty, you were sleeping with her when I came home for Christmas," Molly said, keeping her voice calm and even, despite the anger she still felt. She wanted to get this over with and she wanted Dusty to leave. The best way to achieve that end was to shoot down his dreams of a second chance as swiftly as possible, give him the ring, and say good-bye. "You were sleeping with both of us at the same time. And I didn't ask you to use a condom, because I thought I was sleeping with my future husband. And you sure as hell weren't wearing a condom with her if she convinced you she was pregnant."

The tips of his ears were bright red as he looked out the window.

"How could you do that to me?" she asked, all of the hurt and humiliation from yesterday morning taking center stage in her chest and squeezing. "That was *a horrible* thing to do. You should've just broken up with me at Christmas."

"But I still loved you. I *do* love you."

"You did maybe, once. But you don't anymore. Come on, Dust, you don't and we both know it. You don't treat someone you love like that."

"I was just lonesome, Mol. You were here. I was there. Shana was . . . persuasive." He pulled into the parking lot of her small apartment complex and cut the engine.

"I'm sure," she said, realizing she had no interest in fighting with him. Her chest relaxed and she filled her lungs. "Even if you hadn't slept with Shana, though . . . You live there. I live here. I'm *staying* here."

He sighed, looking around at the suburban apartment complex. "Maybe I could give Philly a try . . ."

"No," she said gently, delivering the final blow. "I don't love you anymore. There's no second chance waiting for you here. This is over. I'm sorry."

He turned to her, shaking his head with tears in his eyes. "I'm a fool, Molly Samaria. Just a damned fool."

"Yes, you are." She nodded. "But if you get back to Hopeview by this afternoon, Shana doesn't ever need to know you were here. Maybe you two can—"

"I don't want Shana," he pouted.

"You must have liked something about her."

Am I trying to convince him to be with her? Good Lord, this is a strange turn of events!

"I don't want to talk about her. I'm just—I'm so sorry, Molly," he said in a broken voice. "I screwed up my whole life."

It shocked the hell out of Molly that tears didn't spring into her eyes. Maybe she'd said good-bye to Dusty in her heart a long time ago. Or maybe Friday night's news had killed any remaining tenderness she felt for him. Or maybe . . . maybe it was just that her heart had already been claimed by someone new. She wasn't sure why, but suddenly she didn't feel angry or sad, she only felt relief. She felt free from Dusty and free to follow her heart.

"You'll see. It's for the best." She reached out and touched Dusty's hand. "Wait here and I'll go get the ring for you, okay?"

Tears were streaming down Dusty's face when he turned to her. "I'm gonna miss you."

She couldn't say the same, so she gave Dusty a grim smile, patting his hand before pulling away. "You're gonna be just fine."

While he waited in the car, she slipped into her apartment. Getting down on her hands and knees she searched the corner of the apartment where she'd hurled the ring, finally finding it keeping the dust bunnies company under her TV stand. Charming wove between her legs, begging for his breakfast.

"I'll be right back," she promised him.

Dusty started the car as she stepped back outside, and rolled down his window so she could drop the ring in his palm.

"That guy looked pretty rich, Mol."

"He is.". . . *but instead of devoting his life to making more money, he's going to do something amazing.*

Her lips tilted up as she thought of him standing up to his father and brothers this morning. Her heart swelled with pride and tenderness as she remembered his eyes cutting to hers before he said his piece.

"That why you want him?"

Dusty's voice pulled her back to reality and she pursed her lips, shaking her head as her patience and compassion for Dusty took a big dip at his insinuation. "Nope."

"I hope he treats you better'n I did."

"I think he will," she answered, then winced, remembering his hurt face and furious eyes right before he punched Dusty in the face. *If we can get things back on track.*

"Take care of yourself, Molly."

"Safe drive home, Dusty," she answered, stepping back on the curb and waving good-bye as he drove away.

When Weston reached the bottom of the stairs, Stratton was waiting for him. His older brother adjusted his glasses, which was a nervous tell, and bobbed his chin down the hall toward their father's office.

"Dad wants to see you. In his study."

Weston nodded, turning in that direction, surprised when Stratton followed him. "You too?"

"All of us," said Stratton grimly.

The door to the study was open and Weston's father sat behind his century-old antique cherry desk. Weston remembered all the times he'd used the desk for a Hide & Seek spot, loving the smells of stale cigar smoke mixed with scotch and leather. He'd been so sure that was the life he wanted for himself too . . . until he wasn't.

Barrett, Fitz, and Alex were all seated on the button-tufted brown leather sofa across from his father's desk and Kate sat in one of the elegant wingback chairs in front of the fireplace. Weston entered the room without making eye contact with anyone and sat down in the free wingback, while Stratton perched on the arm of his chair. He looked expectantly up at his father, wondering what was coming next.

Tom English, who'd still been fairly dashing when he met Weston's mother Eleanora at a ski resort in 1981, looked older now. His graying hair was thinning and his wrinkles seemed deeper. He'd always carried around a gut, despite the way his wife kept after him to play tennis, ride, and swim with regularity. But his eyes had creased laugh lines that had always made him feel approachable, despite his intimidating business acumen and success. He looked up at Weston and sighed.

"So . . . we have our first deserter."

Nobody chuckled at this opening, though Weston wondered if it was meant to lighten the moment. Alex scoffed softly and shot a look to Weston, which Weston felt but didn't return.

"Wes, when you decided to pursue law school, I understood that it was for the purposes of joining me and your brothers at English & Sons. Was I wrong in that assumption?"

"No, sir."

"Yet you aspire to a different career path now, two weeks before the bar."

"Yes, sir."

"I sense this isn't a trivial decision. I sense that you're not just motivated by your brain, but by your heart."

"Yes, sir. I feel strongly about making a difference."

"Not the sort of difference that makes a million or two a year?" his father asked, his face soft as he tented his hands under his chin.

"The money is compelling, but my trust fund will ensure a comfortable life. Whatever employment I seek will simply augment that income."

"True." Tom English sighed again, looking around the study at each of his sons, catching their eyes for a moment before returning to Weston. "You're letting down your brothers."

Weston swallowed. "Which bothers me more than I can express."

"And speaks to your commitment to the DA's office."

Weston's eyes stung suddenly from this unexpected reprieve, and he held his father's eyes with gratitude as Tom continued speaking.

"I'm proud of you, Wes. I'm proud of all my sons, but I'm so damn proud of you for figuring out what you want to do with your life and committing to making it happen. Have you applied yet?"

"N-No, sir."

"I'll put in a call to Seth Garrison, the assistant district attorney. We go all the way back to undergrad."

"Thank you, sir," said Weston, shooting a quick look to Fitz. Of all his brothers, Fitz, who was the only other lawyer presently employed at the company, would be most personally affected by Weston's decision. "What about English & Sons?"

"Oh," said his father, a small grin turning up his lips. "You mean English & Co."

"No, I mean—"

"Well, if Kate comes on board as legal counsel, as she agreed this morning, I can't very well sideline her from the company name, can I? My brother would have a fit."

All five of her cousins whipped their eyes to Kate, who smiled back at her uncle, shaking her head. "You always did have a flair for drama, Uncle Tom!" Looking around at her cousins before stopping on Weston's face, she nodded. "It's true. I accepted the job this morning: chief legal counsel for English & Co., starting in three weeks. I'll need to give notice at my job in New York and tie up some loose ends there, but I'll be moving to Philly in March."

As the room exploded into surprised approval and warm congratulations, Weston took a deep, ragged, relieved breath and felt the weight of the world tumble from his shoulders. He stood, taking two steps to the couch where Kate sat, surrounded by his brothers. Looking up, she grinned and stood. Weston opened his arms and wrapped her in a fond embrace, whispering, "I owe you," in her ear.

"Don't worry," she answered, humor thick in her voice. "I'll remember to collect."

Over Kate's shoulder, Weston caught a glimpse of Alex, his face slowly segueing from anger to acceptance, but Weston still saw disappointment in the blue depths. He knew that it would take a little time for his relationship with Alex to recover, but after watching Alex fly into a rage and hit Dusty this morning, he knew everything would eventually be okay.

As Stratton and Fitz commandeered Kate for a quick conversation about upcoming legal issues, Weston stepped behind his father's desk. His father stood, clasped Weston in a bear hug of an embrace, and clapped his back twice before releasing him.

"Glad we got it all sorted out," he said, grinning at his youngest son.

"I'm relieved, Dad. Thank God for Kate."

"Indeed. And I have to admit, it's high time English & Co. had a woman on board. We don't want to appear sexist, do we? Kate's going to do wonderful things with us, son. And it was . . . well, let's just say Kate was ready for a change, too."

Weston wondered at his father's suddenly thoughtful expression as he looked across the room at his niece, but he didn't pry. Kate was entitled to her secrets . . . at least until she started attending Thursday Nights at Mulligan's when the Edwards sisters, Jessica, Valeria, and . . . and—his face softened as he realized the course of his thoughts—*Molly* started wrangling them out of her.

"Uh-oh. I know that look. Had it plenty when I met your mother. Who *was* that woman at breakfast this morning? Created quite a spectacle."

"Her name's Molly," said Weston, taking a deep breath.

"Can I assume we'll all be seeing more of Molly?"

"If I have my way. I have a date with her tonight, but I'm half tempted to show up at her place right now and put things right."

Tom English nodded. "Sounds like it might get serious."

"Yes, sir," answered Weston without hesitation. "I hope so."

"Then I think you better make a detour to the front parlor first. There's someone waiting there to see you."

Weston started, tilting his head to the side in confusion, but his father gestured toward the parlor with his chin and Weston slipped out of the study unnoticed by his brothers, who were all gathered around Kate.

Someone waiting . . . who? Had Molly come back? He practically ran the rest of the way down the hall.

Pushing open the parlor door, the first thing he noted was the lit fire and silver service of tea on the coffee table. Entering the room softly, he leaned over the high back loveseat where he and Molly had sat together last night to find a softly snoring Connie, still dressed in jeans and a blazer like the last time he saw her. He took his phone out of his back pocket to check the time: a little after eleven o'clock. There's no way she'd come back and forth from Italy. It wasn't possible.

He circled the loveseat and squatted down before her, nudging her shoulder gently.

"Con? Connie?"

Her eyes blinked twice before opening.

"Wes," she breathed, her dreamy voice full of tenderness.

He helped her sit up and she rubbed her eyes, then patted her hair. "Sorry I fell asleep."

Opting for a chair near her instead of sitting beside her, he saw a small wave of disappointment cross her face.

"I can't figure out how you got here."

"I flew to New York yesterday afternoon. I was at Kennedy, waiting for my flight to Rome to be called when I texted you. When you wrote back, wanting to talk today, I cancelled my flight and stayed with my sister, Felicity, in the city. We had a . . . late night." *Late night.* Her voice was suggestive and when she met Weston's eyes, his chest started to tighten as it always did when she baited him like that. "I took a car back this morning."

"Late night, huh?"

"Oh, you know Felicity," she demurred, a coquettish smile hiding whatever she'd done—or not done—last night, dangling noninformation and innuendo in a way that used to make Weston patently crazy.

Used to.

Huh. Used to.

His chest loosened and he took a deep breath.

He didn't care. He didn't care what Connie had been up to and who she'd been up to it with. He didn't want to know or need to know. In fact, he was glad that while he'd been having such an amazing time with Molly, Connie had been enjoying herself too.

"Good for you. Felicity was always fun."

Her grin faded and her eyes searched his face, disappointed and confused. He wasn't giving her the response she'd expected: the pouting, the jealousy, the possessiveness.

"Yes, well. New York boys are *so* . . . you know." She flipped her wrist in the air and reached for her tea cup, watching Weston over the rim.

"Con?"

"Mmm?"

"You were right yesterday. It's not going to happen for us."

She tilted the cup back down as her lips parted in surprise. "But I lov—"

"No, you don't. You don't love me, and I don't love you."

"Yes, darling. I *do* love you."

"Connie, if you loved me, you wouldn't come here trying to make me jealous as a way back into my life. You'd just come and tell me how you felt, but unfortunately, I'd still have to tell you no. We played too many games with each other. We killed whatever could have been good between us."

Her eyes narrowed, and she replaced the cup to her saucer a bit too roughly, rattling the delicate china.

"I canceled my trip to—"

"I didn't ask you to do that," said Weston. "And you're still packed, I assume? I'm sure there's another flight this afternoon."

Her eyes suddenly glistened with tears. "I wanted to give us a chance, Wes. A real chance."

"We're no good for each other, Con," he answered gently, taking her hand and pressing his lips to it in good-bye. He stood, pulling her up with him.

She yanked her hand away, her nostrils flaring and her eyes flinty with anger. "Just another English brother dumping an Atwell sister."

"You're rewriting history."

She lifted her chin. "I don't think so. I think I just beat you to the punch yesterday and today you're having your revenge."

Weston crossed his arms over his chest and took a step back from her like he'd been slapped. "If that's what you really think of me, it's a mystery why you showed up here this morning." He gave her a hard look before turning away and walking to the door. It baffled him to think of what he'd ever seen in her . . . and he felt a sudden deluge of thanks for Molly, whose sweetness and goodness had ensnared his heart before Connie could get her hooks into him again. "Good-bye, Connie. Shall I call you a cab?"

Chapter 16

Molly had settled for *Titanic*, though she wasn't really in the mood to watch it.

After Dusty had driven away, she'd taken a long, hot shower and put on baggy sweats and a worn-out T-shirt that said "Buckeye Girl!" Her damp hair was looped up in a messy bun and she'd eschewed her contacts for glasses. Charming was curled up beside her on the couch and her grandmother's afghan was thrown over her legs, which rested on the coffee table in front of her. She was comfortable, but tired, and wished she could have taken a nap, but her brain was humming with uncomfortable questions, her thoughts an unpleasant cocktail of misgivings and impatience.

Was it a mistake to sleep with Weston last night?

Would he show up at six o'clock for their date or not?

Why would he even want to see her again after the scene Dusty made?

She sighed, flipping over the phone in her left hand and muttering a curse word when the screen showed no new texts. It was after noon now. She and Dusty had left the English estate hours ago, but no word from Weston was making her heart clench.

Three times she'd started a text to him.

The first? *So sorry about this morning. Dusty's headed back to Hopeview. See you later?*

She quickly deleted it. It sounded too cloying.

The second? *I'm so sorry about this morning. Dusty's gone.*

She could practically smell the desperation, so she deleted that one too.

Plus, she'd learned long ago . . . if you didn't ask a question, you couldn't expect a reply and the only thing—the *only* thing—Molly wanted to know was whether or not she'd be seeing Weston again. The thought that he'd pull the plug on their tiny baby of a relationship made her want to weep ugly tears.

The third text? *We still on for later?*

Ugh. She stared at the text for an extra minute, then rolled her eyes and quickly deleted that one too, flipping the over the phone in an attempt to ignore it for a while. They'd left it that he'd come over at six. She'd be ready at six. If he didn't show, she'd have her answer.

As she ignored Kate and Leo racing around the ship holding hands, she thought about all the beautiful things Weston had said to her last night—just for the purpose of torturing herself, of course—and made a list in her head of her favorites:

Thanks for making it not-so-horrible, Molly Samaria McKenna.

He gives up a girl who kisses like you do? He's a douchebag, a jackass, and certifiable.

I think you're amazing.

I follow you willingly every time.

You look lovely in the moonlight, Molly.

It doesn't matter how long ago we met . . . I like you. I think you like me.

It all got horrible again when you left.

I've got a feeling about you, Molly McKenna, my sweet Samaritan. I get the feeling I'd bend for you.

This? Right now? Between us? It's not casual to me, Molly. I don't know where we'll go from here, but I feel like we're at the beginning of something good.

This is just the beginning . . . This is just the beginning . . . This is just the beginning . . .

Those were the words that circled endlessly in her head as she tried to convince herself not to call him, not to text him, just to trust that in five hours her doorbell would ring and he'd be standing there. She had to believe it was true. She had to believe it, because next to her position with Teach for America, she'd never wanted anything else as much in her entire life as Weston English, and the thought of him not showing up was too painful to contemplate.

She sighed again and Charming pricked his ears up, tilting them back and forth like he was listening for something. It always freaked her out when he did that.

"Charming? What do you hear?" she asked, scratching under his chin. His body relaxed and he purred softly, but a moment later, his ears pricked up again, so she shouldn't have been surprised when her doorbell rang.

Weston wasn't convinced that driving her car back to her apartment several hours before their date was the right plan, but any plan that didn't include seeing Molly again as soon as possible was simply wrong.

With a huge slice of wedding cake in one hand and her car keys in the other, he prayed that Dusty would be gone, and Molly would be happy to see him.

What he didn't expect was for her to open the door, cover her mouth with a gasp, and run away.

Stunned but curious, Weston stepped into the apartment and closed the door behind him, walking down the short entry hallway into her living room. *Titanic* was playing on TV, and a large, grumpy-looking cat yawned as Weston caught sight of him.

"Molly?" he called.

Was Dusty here? Was Dusty still here and she'd run to her room to tell him to get dressed? Weston's face flushed uncomfortably. Well, even if that was the case, he still wasn't leaving. He'd fight for a chance with Molly if he had to.

Placing her keys and the cake on her kitchen counter, he shrugged out of his jacket and folded it over one of two bar stools under her kitchen counter, then turned and faced her cat again.

"Where's your mama?" he asked. Then, "Molly?"

"One minute!" she called from behind a door at the opposite side of the small living room.

Feeling awkward and wondering what she was doing, he crossed the living room to knock softly on her bedroom door. "Molly? Please come out."

She finally opened the door and stepped toward him, wearing jeans and a T-shirt that proudly proclaimed her a "Buckeye Girl!" Her hair was loose but damp around her shoulders, and while he thought he'd glimpsed glasses when she opened the door, she was wearing contacts now.

Seeing her made him so happy, he just stood there, saying nothing, smiling at her like she was a present, a surprise, a miracle.

"I didn't expect you," she said, her voice breathy and uncertain.

"I'm early." His eyes lowered to her breasts, then to her jeans. "Did you just go and change for me?"

She nodded. "I was bumming around in sweats."

"Sorry I surprised you," he murmured, reaching for her, grateful when she let him pull her into his arms. "Plus, you look completely beautiful."

Her chest pushed into his as she took several deep breaths, as though her sprint to the bedroom and quick change had winded her. He rubbed his hands over her back and it took him a second to realize that the hitch in her breathing wasn't breath-catching. It was crying.

"Molly?" he whispered, leaning back to look at her face.

"Sorry," she said, her broken voice weak from tears and a sniffle.

"Sweetheart, what's wrong?"

"I didn't . . . I didn't know if you would . . . I mean, if we were . . ."

He took her hand and led her to the sofa, drawing her down beside him. She swiped at her eyes, and he put his arm around her shoulders so she could rest her cheek against his chest.

"You didn't think I was coming?" he asked.

"I did. I mean . . . I wanted to believe it. But this morning was so awful with Dusty and the fight and your face . . ."

"You mean my stomach."

"No," she insisted. "Your face. When I left with Dusty."

"Oh. Yeah," he agreed. "It sucked to see that."

"I just wanted to give him back the ring and say good-bye. I wasn't choosing him over you."

He grinned. Her frankness was so refreshing and reassuring to him. It was something that had been missing from his relationship with Connie. "I know. I knew it then. I just hated seeing you walk away with him. I get jealous sometimes . . . but I'm working on it."

"It's okay. You don't need to be jealous of anything," she said, her tears finished now and her voice stronger. "Sorry for the tears. I do that sometimes . . . when I feel overwhelmed."

"I know," he said, tilting her chin up and dropping his lips to hers in a swift, gentle kiss. "I remember from last night."

Then he kissed her again, slipping his hands to her hips and pulling her onto his lap. He marveled at the way she fit against him, straddling his thighs and wrapping her arms around his neck. Through the thin, worn cotton of her T-shirt, he felt her nipples pebble, pressing against his pecs as she moaned into his mouth. The dozen condoms he'd brought were burning a hole in his back pocket, and he suddenly wondered if a dozen would be enough. The heat they generated with one kiss made him dream of spending all afternoon on her couch, in her bed, buried inside her body every way he could come up with until she begged him for release and they found paradise together over and over again.

But there were a few more things he wanted to say first. Because even though they'd met at a wedding, real life began again today, and his heart demanded that *his* real life, moving forward, included Molly.

His lips glided from her mouth to her cheek, pressing butterfly kisses to her freckles until he paused beside her ear.

"Molly?"

"Huh?"

"Connie stopped by my house this morning." Molly drew back to look at him, and he continued quickly, having no interest in toying with her. "And we said good-bye for good. The only woman I want in my life . . . is you."

Her face erupted into the sweetest smile he'd ever seen as her hands reached up to cup his cheeks.

He swallowed, willing himself not to kiss her again until he'd finished his speech. "I want thunder and lightning. I want my good Samaritan. I want to make a difference. I want to bend. I want to make love to you every day—in a stable, in a bed, on this couch in about five minutes—because I can't imagine my life without you. Or maybe I don't want to, because everything in my life started making sense the moment I met you. And regardless of everything that happened this morning with Dusty and Constance, it's *still* a perfect day because I started it with you and I'm here with you now and you better believe I'm going to end it with you, too.

And I know we only met last night and it was at a wedding, which is probably why everything moved so fast, and I don't know if you want what I want or if last night was just—"

"Weston," she said, her eyes dark brown and luminous as she stared back at him. She leaned forward, her body flush with his, and took his bottom lip between hers, kissing it tenderly before catching his eyes again. "I'm *wild* about you. All you want is me? All I want . . . is *you*."

His eyes closed in relief and a second later he felt the softness of her lips against his eyelids, pressing a kiss to each before skimming over his face like a blessing, like a benediction. He pulled her closer and his heart swelled with emotion—gratitude and tenderness, wonder and love—as he wove his fingers into her hair and poured every feeling he had into their kiss.

He wanted Molly to know—no matter how they met, or where, or when—that his heart was at home with hers.

That he was, and likely always would be, wild about her too.

THE END

The English Brothers continues with …

KISS ME KATE

THE ENGLISH BROTHERS, BOOK #6

THE ENGLISH BROTHERS
(Part I of the Blueberry Lane Series)

Breaking Up with Barrett
Falling for Fitz
Anyone but Alex
Seduced by Stratton
Wild about Weston
Kiss Me Kate
Marrying Mr. English

Turn the page to read a sneak peek of *Kiss Me Kate*!

Chapter 1

From the moment Kate English found out about Étienne Rousseau's accident, she'd been stalking him on Facebook.

What made this especially challenging—and so pathetic it made Kate cringe—was that Étienne Rousseau didn't, in fact, have a Facebook page. So she had essentially been stalking him by proxy via the Facebook page of his younger sister, Jax.

If Jax Rousseau had been curious about a sudden Friend Request from Kate English, she hadn't let on. It was common knowledge in their shared social circle that Kate had recently moved from New York City to Philadelphia, so Jax probably just assumed that Kate was reaching out to her now that she was living locally.

She wasn't.

She was creeping on Jax's brother . . .

. . . which, for myriad reasons, was so nuts even Kate couldn't completely get her head around it. And yet, here she sat, on her lonely bed, at ten o'clock on a Saturday night, lurking on Jax's Facebook page for any mention of Étienne, who had once—a long, long time ago—broken Kate's heart into a million pieces . . . begging the question: Why did she give a damn about Étienne Rousseau? Especially when he'd never given a damn about her.

Kate grabbed her glass of wine off the bedside table and sipped the Pinot Grigio as her index finger continued its snooping and her brain tried unsuccessfully to ignore this nagging question.

The fact of the matter was that Kate didn't have a good answer. She supposed, if she had to come up with something, she'd admit that she'd never totally gotten over him. Like many other women who'd been dumped and forgotten by an ex, she had a compulsive—and, ah-hem, possibly unhealthy—interest in him that was enabled by the ease of social media. Finding out these tiny tidbits about his life was this strange, compulsive weakness. And yes, there was this, too: the only way someone can break your heart into a million pieces is if you gave it to them in the first place, and Kate had done just that. As a gullible and innocent girl, she had believed herself deeply in love with Étienne. (And given him more than her heart.)

And you never really get over your first, she thought bitterly. *Especially when you move back to the city where it all happened.*

Touching the mouse on her laptop gingerly, she scrolled through a series of Jax-selfies taken an hour ago at the same party Kate had been attending: Jax looking dark-haired, dark-eyed, and fierce, hand on a jutted hip in front of a skyscraper-shaped ice sculpture . . . Jax and her twin sister, Mad, pursing their red, shiny lips for the camera . . . Jax posing with one of the Ambler sisters, her index finger caught between her teeth, somehow managing to look both sexy and bored-to-tears at once . . .

Kate kept skating up through pictures and status updates, chuckling softly at a quip about stiletto heels and rainy spring nights. Though they'd been childhood acquaintances,

Kate had only recently gotten to know adult-Jax through a month's worth of lurking, and she liked the feisty young brunette. Plus, Jax updated her Facebook account about twenty times a day, which meant that mentions of Étienne, while occasional, still popped up a couple times a week to feed Kate's obsession.

Peeking at the laptop screen over the rim of her glass as she took another sip of wine, Kate almost missed what she was looking for. Her eyes widened and she jerked her finger on the mouse, scrolling back down quickly. Changing her sip to a gulp, she read Jax's status from earlier today:

Jacqueline "Jax" Rousseau: *Big Bro getting his cast off tomorrow! Gird your loins, females of Philly. Ten'll be back in action soooooon, bitches!*

Staring at the screen, Kate read the post three more times before snapping the laptop closed and swinging her legs over the side of her bed with disgust. She huffed softly, causing Oliver, her latest rescue cat, to leap off the bed and hide beneath it, while Annie, the marmalade tabby she'd rescued two years ago, gave Kate the stink eye from the end of the bed for disrupting her sleep.

Kate's baggy pajama bottoms whooshed softly as she marched through the halls of her rented condo, heading for the kitchen to refill her wine glass.

"Gird your loins," she muttered to Cinderella, a blue-eyed Himalayan who followed her mistress to the kitchen. Kate was fostering her until the local shelter could find a family equipped to care for an HIV-positive feline.

Kate's contact at PAWS for LOVE had called again this morning to ask if she could foster one more, and while Kate hated to say no, she had no choice but to refuse. Until she had a house of her own with some grounds to build a small kennel for orphans and strays, her condo couldn't accommodate another body. Not to mention, one more cat and she'd be approaching "crazy cat lady" territory, which was a little too close to the truth for Kate to bear.

Looking down at the pretty gray and white kitten, Kate huffed derisively, "Back in action, huh? Back to whoring, more like. Oh, I wish I'd never met I him. I wish I'd never even known how it felt . . ."

Cinderella meowed as Kate's voice trailed off. Wishes were futile. She *had* met him. She *did* know. She couldn't *unknow* the feeling of being with Étienne, but she wished she could somehow forget it.

Pursing her lips and bracing her hands on the kitchen counter, she bowed her head in frustration, grappling for strength and direction. Although it was impossible to turn back time and make different choices, she was a strong, smart woman and she could certainly take control of her behavior *now*. Promising herself—for the hundredth time— that she'd unfollow Jax and stop cyber-stalking Étienne on Facebook, she turned her back to the counter, leaning against it and crossing her arms over her chest.

After all, thought Kate, *it really isn't fair to Tony.*

Tony Reddington, the son of her father's business partner, had been kind enough to take Kate out for din- ner when she'd first relocated to Philadelphia, and had turned into a pseudo-boyfriend of sorts. Her go-to escort for parties and galas, Tony was well-educated, cultured, charming, and always gracious, filling their evenings with amusing observations and witty conversation. When he picked up Kate in his shiny Mercedes, he always had flow- ers waiting, and when he dropped her off at the end of their dates, he never groped or pushed, opting for a chaste kiss on the lips instead, followed by a playful wink and a promise to call her. A promise he always kept.

Tony was a gentleman of the highest order and Kate knew that she should be blissfully happy on his arm, with the possibility of long-awaited wedding bells echoing in her head.

So, what was the problem?

Kate's cheeks flushed as she considered the shameful answer.

After six weeks of delightful conversation, gorgeous flowers, and chaste kisses, Kate wanted more . . . but not necessarily from Tony. Kate's dirty little secret was that she couldn't shake memories of Étienne since returning to Philly. She wanted hot, wet, sweet, filthy kisses that would make her toes curl. She wanted fingers that burned her skin like fire, lips that sucked until she screamed, and a tongue that could make stars burst behind closed eyes. She wanted thick and hot sliding into her core over and over again until her body tensed and strained, finally exploding into a million pieces of delight, only pulled back to earth and put back together by lips that sought hers hungrily all. over. again.

As far as Kate was concerned, that kind of burning and cooling, falling apart and coming together, sweet and filthy only existed in one man—the one man with whom Kate had ever experienced all of those things at once: Étienne Rousseau.

Kate's body wanted him bad.

Which was a shame, because Étienne Rousseau was also the one man on earth that Kate English could never, ever have. Not ever again. Not if she had any self-respect whatsoever.

Buzz. Buzzbuzz.

She glanced at her phone, jolted out of her reverie, placing cool palms on hot cheeks.

Stratton. Hmm.

Kate's cousin, Stratton English, had looked pretty content when Kate and Tony left him at the benefit an hour ago. Cozy in a corner with his new girlfriend, Valeria, he'd appeared more socially comfortable than Kate had ever seen him . . . and that was saying something, since Stratton loathed parties.

She pressed Talk. "Why are you calling me? Why aren't you at home making out with Val?" Waiting for his answer, she cradled the phone between her ear and shoulder, opening the frig door.

He chuckled softly. "It's on the agenda." Then he got quiet, his voice taking on a slight edge. "Are *you* busy? Is, uh, Tony there?"

Yeah, right.

Kate picked up the bottle on the door and kicked the refrigerator door closed. She thought about asking Stratton if he thought it was normal for a guy to stay in the "chaste kiss" zone after six weeks of dating, but she just wasn't in the mood to talk about it. Her cousins, Stratton especially, who were very protective of Kate, approved of Tony and would have no issue with Tony moving as slow as molasses indefinitely. This was a far better conversation for her close girlfriends, who included her cousins' wives, fiancées, and girlfriends.

She pursed her lips as she set the bottle on the counter.

No, not them either. They'd all go home and share Kate's question with their significant others and her cousins would end up weighing in anyway. No. She didn't need advice. Things would eventually heat up, right? She just needed to give Tony a little more time to make his move . . . and in the meantime, she needed to stop letting thoughts of Étienne get her all hot and bothered.

Unfollow Jax. Unfollow Jax. For the love of Pete, unfollow Jax.

Kate rolled her eyes "Nope. He was a perfect gentleman." *Like always.*

"Glad to hear it," said Stratton, edge gone.

"So, what's up?" she asked, uncorking the half-drunk bottle of wine. "Are you still at the party?"

"Yes," he said, and his voice instantly got more serious. "Hey . . . are you sitting down?"

"Nope. But I'm drinking. Will that do?"

"I guess it'll have to," said Stratton.

"Why are you using your doomsday voice, cuz?"

"Because . . . well, for starters, I'm pissed at Barrett."

"Huh." Barrett was Stratton's oldest brother and the CEO of English & Company where Kate worked as a lawyer and Stratton was the acting CFO. Since Stratton was incredibly loyal to his brothers and a generally easygoing person, if he was upset with Barrett, there was a good chance it was work related. "I thought we all agreed, no work at parties."

"A rule Barrett disregards at every turn, at every party, every weekend."

This was true. When it came to business, the only "off" button Barrett knew was his fiancée, Emily Edwards. Otherwise, business was always on the table.

"And usually you don't care."

"This time I do."

Kate grinned. "Okay. Cut to the chase . . . what company did Barrett just agree to buy?"

Stratton sighed heavily. "Here's the deal—no, wait. Before I say anything else, I want you to know . . . we're going to fix this, Kate. I promise."

Kate grimaced lightly, then took a swig directly from the bottle before recorking it and putting it back in the fridge. This was suddenly sounding a little more serious.

If Kate was a classic optimist with closet stalker tendencies, her favorite cousin, Stratton, was a classic fixer with extreme tunnel vision when it came to those he loved. Kate understood Stratton's compulsion to "fix" things for the people he loved, because she would—literally—*do* anything for the people she cared about.

In fact, she thought, thinking of her hot laptop and cold, ungirded loins, that was probably why she couldn't stay away from Jax's Facebook page.

Despite the years between Kate's fleeting week with Étienne and now—despite the way he'd hurt her so long ago—the second she'd heard about Étienne's accident, she'd irrationally longed to race to his bedside and hold his hand. She wasn't under any illusion about his feelings for her. He'd *never* really cared for her—his actions had made that abundantly clear long ago. Hell, at this point, she didn't even know if he still *remembered* her—she hadn't seen him or heard from him in over twelve years, and in that twelve years, by all accounts, Étienne hadn't been lonely.

But even at fifteen years old, Étienne Rousseau was more irreverent and untouchable than anyone Kate had ever met, which pretty much made him the brooding nip to Kate's curious cat. Back then, in addition to his lips on hers and his hands all over her body, she'd wanted to connect with him, understand him, matter to him, belong to him. Instead— she remembered, stiffening her spine—he took her virginity and she never saw his face again.

Suddenly she had a sharp sense of foreboding as she turned back to the conversation. "You're making me nervous, Strat."

"I don't know how this happened, but . . . Barrett just got into bed with the Rousseau Trust," he blurted out.

Look for *Kiss Me Kate* at your local bookstore or buy online!

Other Books by Katy Regnery

A MODERN FAIRYTALE

(Stand-alone, full-length, unconnected romances inspired by classic fairy tales.)

The Vixen and the Vet
(inspired by "Beauty and the Beast")
2014

Never Let You Go
(inspired by "Hansel and Gretel")
2015

Ginger's Heart
(inspired by "Little Red Riding Hood")
2016

Don't Speak
(inspired by "The Little Mermaid")
2017

Swan Song
(inspired by "The Ugly Duckling")
2018

ENCHANTED PLACES

(Stand-alone, full-length stories that are set in beautiful places.)

Playing for Love at Deep Haven
2015

Restoring Love at Bolton Castle
2016

Risking Love at Moonstone Manor
2017

A Season of Love at Summerhaven
2018

ABOUT THE AUTHOR

USA Today **bestselling author Katy Regnery** started her writing career by enrolling in a short story class in January 2012. One year later, she signed her first contract for a winter romance entitled *By Proxy*.

Katy claims authorship of the multi-titled Blueberry Lane Series which follows the English, Winslow, Rousseau, Story and Ambler families of Philadelphia, the five-book, best-selling A Modern Fairytale series, the Enchanted Places series, and a standalone novella, *Frosted*.

Katy's first Modern Fairytale romance, *The Vixen and the Vet*, was nominated for a RITA® in 2015 and won the 2015 Kindle Book Award for romance. Four of her books: *The Vixen and the Vet* (A Modern Fairytale), *Never Let You Go* (A Modern Fairytale), *Falling for Fitz* (The English Brothers #2) and *By Proxy* (Heart of Montana #1) have been #1 genre bestsellers on Amazon. Katy's boxed set, The English Brothers Boxed Set, Books #1–4, hit the *USA Today* bestseller list in 2015 and her Christmas story, *Marrying Mr. English*, appeared on the same list a week later.

Katy lives in the relative wilds of northern Fairfield County, Connecticut, where her writing room looks out at the woods, and her husband, two young children, and two dogs create just enough cheerful chaos to remind her that the very best love stories begin at home.

Sign up for Katy's newsletter today: http://www.katyregnery.com!

Connect with Katy

Katy LOVES connecting with her readers and answers every e-mail, message, tweet, and post personally! Connect with Katy!

Katy's Website: http://katyregnery.com
Katy's E-mail: katy@katyregnery.com
Katy's Facebook Page: https://www.facebook.com/KatyRegnery
Katy's Pinterest Page: https://www.pinterest.com/
    katharineregner
Katy's Amazon Profile: http://www.amazon.com/
    Katy-Regnery/e/B00FDZKXYU
Katy's Goodreads Profile: https://www.goodreads.com/author/
    show/7211470.Katy_Regnery

CPSIA information can be obtained at www.ICGtesting.com
Printed in the USA
LVOW08s0313200416

484247LV00003B/4/P